Nudity in a Public Place

Nudity in a Public Place

JOHN NETTLES

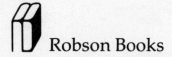

Robson Books

First published in Great Britain in 1991 by
Robson Books Ltd, Bolsover House, 5–6
Clipstone Street, London W1P 7EB

Illustrations by John Jensen

**British Library Cataloguing in Pub-
lication Data**
Nettles, John, 1948–
    Nudity in a public place.
    I. Title
    791.45028092

ISBN 0 86051 764 0

Typeset and printed in Great Britain by
Butler & Tanner, Frome and London

This book is dedicated to Robert 'the Laird' Banks Stewart, who knew me when I was nothing, and still does.

Contents

Introduction

Prepared I was not. I was, as the Americans say, a 'tights' actor, playing to largely middle-class audiences who, while duly and properly appreciative of my artistry, remained small in number. There was little or no danger of being recognized by children in the street, accosted by damp matriarchs or waylaid by foetid hacks from the spiritual wasteland of Wapping.

Though I could call Peter Brook by his first name and on a good day he would remember mine, it was none the less true that Mr and Mrs J. Public could not have given a flying act of congress who I was or what I did, whom I loved or whom I loathed. My privacy was secure, taken for granted; my obscurity was almost complete. However, all this was to change.

The creator of the *Bergerac* series, an ebullient Scot glorying in the name of Robert Banks Stewart – or 'The Laird', as he was dubbed – gave me no hint of what was about to happen. He merely said that I was to play a humble detective

"The Laird"

working the beat on the Isle of Jersey (a place I had visited once, in 1969, appearing in an Ingmar Bergman play of such monstrous pretension and in such monstrously pretensious mauve tights that I prefer to forget the experience). The programme was designed to take over from *Shoestring*, the star of which, Trevor Eve, had left to become an even bigger star in the Los Angeles firmament. So it was that another sensitive thespian walked a little hesitantly from the shadows on to a million television screens.

Sounds good, doesn't it? Well ... Despite being in my own estimation (and that of my mother) God's finest gift to the theatre, my first stab at the 'Bergerac' character proved almost fatal. The Laird showed me the opening day's rushes. I had not seen myself much on screen before and it was a dispiriting experience, due not so much to the quality of the tape – which made me and everything around me a bilious yellow-green colour – as to the quality of my performance, which was horribly overstated and dreadfully melodramatic. What I had fondly imagined to be a fine and subtle display of controlled anger in the face of bureaucratic oppression was, in fact, like nothing so much as the tantrum of a small boy deprived of his pocket money for shaving the dog. Worst of all was the accent – well suited to any Shakespearean king but totally out of place in the mouth of a Jersey detective, or any other detective. The Laird, with commendable if uncharacteristic restraint, said I sounded like Prince Charles, opining that it be a good career move if I found a different voice for the part. It was, and I did.

But there was more trauma to be endured before I could scale the giddy heights of mini-celebdom and be able to talk to Lionel Blair on equal terms or appear on *Call My Bluff*. Everybody involved in the making of the programme was supportive; at least, when I was in earshot they were optimistic as to the success of the venture. They might even have believed it in their heart of hearts, but they could not know for certain. I heard (by accident, dear reader, by accident) one lady quite intimately connected with the production of the show – noted, it must be said, more for the size of her chest than her critical acumen – remark to her lover that while I was quite a pleasant chap, she didn't believe the series would be a success. I half believed her.

At the end of filming, my ego having taken something of a battering, I was extremely tired; like Steve Bisley, who went through a similar experience with *Call Me Mister*, I could have slept on barbed wire. I gratefully accepted an offer from the RSC to appear in *La Ronde*, although this was possibly a mistake. *La Ronde* is a gloomy play, with no discernible dramatic merit whatsoever – which is surprising when you consider that each little scene ends with a bout of explicit love-making (in our production, directed by John Barton, congress was always conducted missionary style – man on top. My timorous suggestion that we ring a few changes on this theme was greeted with, I thought, rather hurtful coldness but then, given my experience with the Jersey detective, I was a little over-sensitive.) Be that as it may, this Mogadon production was not successful. Patrons fell asleep, left noisily, didn't bother to turn up at all. I managed to get a couple of ambiguously worded reviews which could have been interpreted as praise, but I rather believe that the critics had left long before I appeared in the final two scenes and simply gave me the benefit of the doubt.

It wasn't a happy time. I was overtaken by bouts of maudlin self-pity and self-doubt, my paranoia fuelled by an excessive intake of alcohol and nicotine. Things had to get better, and they did. On a night when I had almost garrotted myself on stage trying to get a recalcitrant cloak unfastened, the better to make love to Barbara Leigh Hunt, someone showed me the ratings for *Bergerac*. They were more than good; they were marvellous. This was due in no small measure to clever scheduling, *Bergerac* appearing together with *To the Manor Born* and *Mastermind* – Sunday night belonged to the BBC. It was a success.

A new series was planned and slowly and surely I found myself becoming a mini-celebrity, henceforward MC. Children did hoot at me in the street; predatory females of uncertain years did press themselves upon me, literally and metaphorically; and Fleet Street's finest suddenly found my private life of extraordinary and compelling interest. As final and positive proof that I had arrived and was indeed an MC, I was ushered willy-nilly into an amazing world, peopled by showbiz personalities, famous for being famous, liars, cheats, con-men, journalists both good and bad, comics, dancers, charity workers, fellow MCs all jostling together in a mad, mad world of hype and pretence, of extraordinary vulgarity and indescribable tackiness; but occasionally, and surprisingly, a world of great love, laughter and beauty. What follows is the story of my experiences in that world. Welcome to it.

1
The Beginning

'... prologues to the swelling act ...'
Macbeth

I did not seem destined for glory; the mark of future fame
was not indelibly imprinted on my brow. In fact, my beginnings were distinctly inauspicious to say the least. My real
parents I never knew. They omitted to get married, before,
during or even after producing me, and then they went their
separate ways, leaving me in the loving care of two very
splendid people who adopted me and became my mum and
dad. I still think of them as such.

I was brought up in Cornwall, an area not exactly
renowned for things theatrical. In fact, I could number my
fellow Cornish thespians on the fingers of one hand after a
mowing accident. Nevertheless, there were a few, a very few,
early indications that I was going to be a star so great that I
would appear with Russell Grant and Joan Collins. There
was my first appearance as one of the wood elves in a drama,
daringly set in the round, performed at Par Drill Hall. It is
true that due to the pressures of the occasion, I was taken a
little short and could not quite say the words properly with

my legs so tightly crossed, but the luscious Miss Coombes, who tucked her dress provocatively in her knickers when she took PE, said them for me. It was clear even then, as my mother said, long, long years after, that I was destined for celebrity.

I did not care too much one way or the other at this stage, as I was busy enjoying life as 'a child of the clay'. St Austell, where I lived in Cornwall, was the heart of clay country. The precious white stuff was blasted and washed clear of the great cliff faces of the open-cast mines, hurled down through the races into the settling tanks and from there taken to the fearsome dries, where men, stripped to the waist and looking like wedding cakes, sweated and strained in awful heat to turn the sodden lumps of clay into dust so fine that a stone might sink in it. From the linhays, where it was stored, the precious clay was taken by roaring lorries and huffing steam trains to the ports of Charlestown, Par and Fowey, to be shipped to places far beyond my world.

The evidence of this mighty, never-ending endeavour lay everywhere. The trees, the hedgerows, the bushes and the very flowers were hung about with a ghostly white film, an everlasting hoar frost. The brooks and rivers ran a milky-white effluent down to St Austell Bay, turning the sea between the Dodman Point and Gribbin Head a most beautiful and beguiling turquoise colour. Holidaymakers thought this the handiwork of God; the good and circumspect Cornish were not about to disabuse them of the notion. But greater than all this were the soaring pyramids of clay waste, atop the great granite masses stretching up across Roche Rock and northward to Indian Queens. Clinging to the pillion of my father's fork-sprung antique motorbike as we hammered to the top of windy Penpillick Hill, I could see them dancing through my tears, ranged mighty and black against the dazzle of the setting sun. Later, when we were braver, we scapegrace lads would forage on the banks of these gargantuan waste heaps for pieces of that most beautiful of purple quartzes, which we carried off home as trophies and proofs of great courage.

Though my father was a carpenter, most of my little friends' fathers were in the clay, as we used to call it. They were grave, remote men and a little frightening to me. Their skins were porcelain white through lack of sunlight and their eyes red-rimmed and raw from the endless dust. The clay was ingrained in every pore, crease and wrinkle. They all smoked Woodbines, Weights or thin roll-ups and almost without exception appeared to suffer from some unforgiving illness that sapped their powers of speech and movement – many died years before their time because of cancers and chronic chest complaints. They were always distantly kind to me and, as was only right and proper, I was distantly respectful of them, these men who knew the secret of the claymine, linhay and dry, where I had never been.

Not that I thought too much about all this at the time, or about one little boy, Peter Elliot, who cried from sheer cold one bleak, dark winter's day because his clothes were little more than rags. His father, fresh from the night shift, covered in clay, came to the school to remonstrate in dignified fashion with a strangely unkind teacher who had singled out his son in front of the whole school for being so badly dressed. I didn't think much of it then, but I remember it well enough now.

I had an excuse for not heeding these seminal experiences, and the excuse, as you might have guessed, dear reader, was of course a woman. I was in love, hopelessly and helplessly in love with Barbara Gillespie. Her father ran the pub just outside the school gates and she was beautiful, even more beautiful than the heroines in my Mabel Lucy Attwell annual, with her long blonde hair, the palest of pale blue eyes, small perfect teeth and winning smile.

I was not an MC at the time, and the problem was not so much how to win her as how to get her to notice me at all. The best time had to be Miss Coombes's music and movement class, when we were all sorted out, as far as was possible, into boy–girl pairs. I would make my play then. I could not hope to win her as my rich friend Ben Lyons might, with promises of the small but delicious penny ice lollies from Mr Arnold's little shop at lunchtime. Nor could I hope to compete with the darkly handsome Peter Cox as far as looks were concerned. I would have to rely on my native wit and charm.

On the morning of the class, I rose specially early, scrubbed my face with panshine and an ancient loofah and combed my hair carefully, using Brylcreem to give it that extra lustre. Aglow with a quite novel cleanliness and wearing a new Aertex shirt with short sleeves, matching khaki shorts and a much-polished pair of open-toed sandals, I set out for school, accompanied by my mother and her sister, Aunty Bertha (who has since changed her name to Betty for reasons I can only guess at). We went down the steep and narrow lane from Seaview Terrace, high above St Blazey, where we lived. Towards the bottom of the lane, near Kittows the butchers (they now call themselves meat surgeons!), we encountered a large herd of cows wending their way slowly and thoughtfully up the lane to their pasture. They passed us by. My head fuller of amorous ambition than present care, I slipped on a large cowpat and was instantly engulfed in the viscous ordure. My mother rushed me back to our little house and performed some hasty restoration work – it had to be hasty as she needed to get to work herself quite shortly – but it wasn't quite hasty enough. I was late for school. The music and movement class had already commenced and the awful if handsome Cox was sitting confidently by my wondrous Barbara, wheedling his way, easily it seemed, into her affections. With a courage born of misfortune, I marched straight across the room, sat on her other side and tried to engage her in conversation. She inquired with heart-stopping grace why my shirt and shorts were wet and my shoes caked with what she took to be mud. I gave an honest account of my heroic and certainly dangerous encounter with the forces of unyielding nature. Her response was extraordinary. Instead of offering me sympathy and perhaps squeezing my hand just a little, she held her nose between finger and thumb, emitted strange whooping sounds and leapt off to the other side of the room, followed almost immediately by the hateful Cox. This was bad enough, but further desperate humiliation followed. Miss Coombes turned against me and chose Cox and my Barbara to lead the final dance. Because there were more boys than girls, and because news had spread of my bovine encounter, I was forced to dance with the unsightly Freddie Jones, noted for nothing so much as his perpetually running nose. In despair, I looked up at my old friend Phyllis Banbury. She might not have been quite so pretty as Barbara, but she lived on a farm, had a proper gang, tore her skirt along the seams so she could run faster and bit chunks out of loaves of bread and swore to her mother it was the mice; she did not mind farming smells one little bit. Away I leapt, and ran across the green fields and forgot, at least briefly, about Peter Cox and the perfidious Barbara.

Despite this personal setback, my progress towards celebrity continued. I landed the plum role of Prince Charming in *Sleeping Beauty*, performed in the back hall of St Blazey's

Methodist church. Aunty Bertha, a notable performer herself (her rendition of 'Some Enchanted Evening' in the St Blazey Amateur Operatic Society's production of *South (west) Pacific*, had been encored twice by Uncle Stan), gave me the benefit of her experience. She also made me a charming, short velvet cloak after the Elizabethan manner, held on by two velvet strips which crossed over my chest and tied in a bow in the small of my back. My sword was a long, painted bamboo stick which, when I remembered, I swaggeringly wore at a very sharp angle to my hip. I acquitted myself very well, I am told, though I had not at that tender age quite mastered the art of kissing properly, nor that of turning quickly on my heel while wearing a sword. I somehow got the thing between my legs, which occasioned me no little pain and caused me to fall over rather suddenly. I reasoned that the audience would take this to be a dramatically viable swooning away after being overcome at the joy of seeing my loved one awake. Whether they did or not, we were all rapturously applauded at the curtain call and I saw my way clear to early stardom.

However, the ladder to success seemed at this juncture to lack a few rungs, for I made no more serious advance towards international fame until my middle teens. You will find this difficult to believe, I know, but when you consider what an MC I later became, intimations of immortality seemed curiously absent during this interim.

Fortunately, my upward career was reactivated by no less a person than Frederick Farnham Flower, a new teacher who took over and reshaped my grammar school, making it less like a seaside borstal and more like an educational establishment. Not since Monmouth had there been such a revolution, and this one was successful. He taught us that there was life beyond Plymouth, that there were honourable alternatives to working in the clay, and that you didn't necessarily have to be effeminate to stop playing football and to like poetry and the arts. He also, bravely, gave me the role of Macbeth when I was fifteen. It is possible that I did not understand as perfectly as I might the finer points of the man's psychology, and certainly the finer points of verse-speaking eluded me, but I knew a good fight when I saw one and I almost beat Macduff on more than one occasion. The visiting schools would cheer me to the very echo as, clothed in a conical steel helmet fashioned by the senior metalwork class and wielding a sword from Nathans, I accounted for a good half-dozen willing third-formers before putting paid, to the accompaniment of even more cheers, to the hapless young Siward. Yes indeed, I was going to be a celebrity. I had the sharp tang of ambition in my mouth and stars bursting in my head. I would not play for England after all, even if they begged me to; I would play the theatre instead, and that right famously.

I had never seen a stage play in my life. To Bristol went your writer, hungry for opportunity, to audition for the National Youth Theatre. Of course, I would play Henry V for them in a forthcoming production in London. In a draughty church hall, my school mac thrown loosely over my shoulders, I gave Michael Croft the benefit of my 'Tomorrow and tomorrow and tomorrow' speech. I had perfected, during the short run of the play at school, a clever way of intensifying the emotions that the words did not adequately convey. I would say a line, pause, and then repeat the same line just to ram it home. This made the speech twice as long and, of course, twice as impressive and moving. He turned me down flat, making some remarks which I thought were quite offensive. I gave up, turning instead to smoking, the love of a good woman and writing free verse about terminal despair, very much in vogue at the time.

My heartbreak and disillusion were increased at the time by my failure in another direction – it seemed that I was not fated to be an internationally acclaimed pop star, or even a pop singer quite well known in mid-Cornwall. All the bits and pieces that went to make up a pop star I had, even in abundance. The hair, for instance, I could cajole into a reasonable likeness of Elvis Presley's by the application of a cunning mixture of Vaseline and Brylcreem, which gave at once firmness and gloss, one strand falling provocatively across the forehead. It's true that I hadn't enough facial hair to make one, let alone two, decent sideboards, but I discovered that if I combed part of the sides of my hair forward and then down, sticking them with the afore-mentioned Vaseline, a creditable result could be achieved.

I came a bit of a cropper, though, over the *de rigueur* black shirt. I asked my mother if I could have a new shirt and she agreed. Off I went to the Co-op in Fore Street and bought a lovely black one which I fondly imagined would look terrific on an international pop star. Mother looked at it once and made me, nay forced me to, take it back, muttering darkly about not having endured the war to have her son dress like a Nazi. I compromised by getting a very, very dark blue version. Still, it was not enough to ensure my success. My failure was due in no small measure to two factors. First, the boys who already had guitars and knew how to convert wireless sets into loudspeakers operated a closed shop when it came to the formation of groups. Second, and more import-antly, I was completely unable to sing. This is something I now freely admit. When my emotional version of 'Donna' was played back to me, I was amazed. I had thought in performance at the Youth Club that I sounded very much like Marty Wilde, only better. I was mistaken. The voice that issued from the speaker sounded like some poor cat caught in a barbarous medieval trap, howling its last of life to a deaf universe.

I betook myself to university in Southampton, devoting myself to the pursuit of history, philosophy and pretty young women, but not necessarily in that order. It was the 1960s, a good time to be young; the only voices to be heard seemed to be those of young people. The youth culture, fatuous and all-embracing, was upon us. So-called stars, possessed of no virtue other than the fact that they could stand up in front of a microphone, were much sought after by the media, to the exclusion of wiser, graver voices. Pop singers provided the philosophy of the age – that power came from the sound of a guitar and insight from half an ounce of grass. We worshipped the golden calves so thoughtfully provided by Hugh Heffner, Bob Dylan, the endlessly angry John Osborne and, of course, The Beatles. It wasn't our parents that fucked my generation up; it was this great pantheon of genius. Some of us might have died trying to live up to their impossibly high ideals, but did we have fun, dancing down the primrose path of unbridled self-indulgence to the middle years of spiritual dereliction.

Yes, it was fab. Even fabber were the occasional visits to my university of the Oxford Playhouse Company. These visits were the highlight of my – and, I suspect, many other people's – year down in Southampton. They were truly wonderful productions and I hold them among my dearest memories. I would cut lectures and sneak into the back of the darkened auditorium of the Nuffield Theatre to watch surreptitiously as the company rehearsed. And what a company it was: Judi Dench, beautiful and gifted beyond all telling, the equally talented Avril Elgar, Barbara Jefford, John Turner, John Hurt, Roger Livesey *et al.* – a company to dream of. I sat mesmerized throughout a performance they gave of *The Three Sisters* and cried unfashionably at the agony of the play, at that strange dance of unbearable innocence and deceit, provincialism and defeated idealism, that turns inexorably into a dance of death to the still, sad music of humanity. I didn't hang around after the shows, as was my wont, to chat with my peers about how we had all understood the play quite easily and to criticize in lordly fashion the performers and their performances. Instead I rushed back to my little room in University Crescent, to cry some more and to read and reread the play in an effort to re-create in my mind the experience I had had in the theatre. It was and still is, some twenty-five years on, very easy to do, and for this I am grateful.

I had to get back to the stage. I actually played Hamlet for the University Players, but the performance was not a resounding success. My father for one was not impressed. I heard him snoring as I delivered 'To be or not to be'. Jocelyn Powell, the highly strung director, told me that my see-through nylon tights were distracting some of the young girls in the school parties. I slipped on the onions that Laertes had taken into Ophelia's grave, the better to make him cry, and I failed utterly to carry out the director's instructions *vis-à-vis* Gertrude, the Queen, my mother, at the very end of the drama. Jocelyn was convinced that Hamlet had an Oedipus complex and that the real drama concerned just two people – the prince and his mum. To emphasize this he directed me in the final act to lift her dead body into my arms, carry her up the steps and seat her on the throne, from where Claudius had but lately been so ignominiously hurled.

Now, I have always considered it unfair that Shakespeare so often asks his tragic heroes to perform so physically at the end of what can be very long plays indeed. Poor King Lear, usually quite an old buffer, has to act his way through some of the most difficult and emotionally draining speeches known to man, and then at the very end of this ordeal is required to carry Cordelia from backstage to forestage, speaking the whilst. God help him if he forgets the exact number of 'howls' to exclaim. Macbeth likewise spends a couple of hours having an awful lot of trouble with witches and wives, bloody ghosts and unbelieving thanes, and on top of all this is required to fight with Macduff – usually a younger actor who has spent most of the play doing nothing more strenuous than sip a can of lager while lounging on his couch reading the *Stage* newspaper. But most unfair of all is Hamlet. The dear boy has to sort out a ghost problem, go mad to just the right degree, shout a lot at his poor mother, deliver soliloquies that ten to one the audience knows much better than he does and then, right at the end, has to fight a long and arduous duel with Laertes – usually a younger actor who has spent most of the play doing nothing more strenuous etc., etc.

So, in Jocelyn's production I had not only to fight and vanquish Laertes, which I could do with a little effort, but then to lift the Queen to the throne, which I couldn't do even with the greatest of effort. Now, Rosemary, who was playing Gertrude, was a great person in many ways. She was beautiful in an English rose sort of way and she had the most marvellous ample breasts I've ever seen. In fact, she was a big girl all round. I, on the other hand, was a weed, a nine-stone amateur thespian, dedicated to juvenile dissipation, who had just been through rather a lot. I tried. Dear God, I tried. I heaved Rosemary's inert mass into my arms and lurched a few steps upstage, uttering the lines 'Heaven make thee free of it, I follow thee.' But then, on the next line, 'I am dead, Horatio', which I might just as well have been, and which I delivered in a near falsetto, I found myself staggering backwards, unable to bear Rosemary's great weight. I fell.

Rosemary's long and many-petticoated dress covered my face entirely; indeed, it covered most of my body. Not able to see, I panicked. The next line, 'Wretched Queen adieu', was delivered from the region of Rosemary's crutch. Horatio, may God bless him, rescued me from Rosemary's body press by dragging her to one side. Thinking discretion the better part of valour, I lay there, codpiece askew and winded, and essayed the rest of my speech. I needn't have bothered. Far from being pale and trembling at this chance, or indeed but mute to the act, the audience was falling about in paroxysms of mirth. I could see my mother indulging in unseemly laughter. My father wasn't joining in, but only because he had just that minute been woken up by the pandemonium and did not know what was going on.

Things could only get better, and luckily they did. My next theatrical outing was in *Caligula*, our entry for the National Students Drama Festival, and we actually won the competition, due in no small measure to the help I received from Kenneth Haig, who had just appeared in the definitive production of that play in London and New York. Harold Hobson, admittedly no stranger to fulsome hyperbole, thought I was all right. The *Guardian* critic was suitably admiring of my efforts, writing at the very end of his review: 'John Nettles gives a very good performance.' A Very Good Performance – I ran the words over and over in my mind like a mantra. How right the perspicacious critic was to recognize one's genius, and what attitude should the recipient of such praise adopt? Should I go to the RSC or the National? (I actually chose winsome self-effacement and went to the Royal Court.) Later I was shown a fuller version of that *Guardian* review. It had been shortened for the

I fell.

London editions and read: 'John Nettles gives a very good performance in parts by students' standards, but it is a pity, if understandable, that as yet he has but little stage technique.'

It is truly very splendid to become famous and to earn a decent living after years of grovelling around in your turn-ups for the price of the next tin of beans. But one must never forget that it is, of course, largely by luck that celebrity comes a-knocking at one's rented door, and it is salutary to remember those days of want, the better to appreciate the days of plenty. I do remember those times of penury and penny-pinching painfully and very clearly. And I remember too those early experiences of theatre.

I will not bore you too much with a detailed account of my early thespian life but will recount just enough to let you understand something of my formative experiences, which go a long way towards explaining the person I have become. I was pitched from the indulgent groves of academe into the Royal Court Theatre at the behest of Bill Gaskill, who thought he might have observed a glimmer of talent about my person. I was grateful and very underpaid.

The theatre was putting on *Macbeth*, which even to my limited understanding is one of the most fiendish (literally) and complex plays in the world to produce successfully, largely because it is so difficult to chart in accessible human terms Macbeth's descent into that murderous maelstrom. It is too easy to make him an outsized monster, blood-spattered and brutish, a thuggish psychopath with whom it is imposs-ible to emphathize. I have seen many productions of this play, which holds a kind of weary fascination for me, but I have only ever seen it work satisfactorily once, in the Trevor Nunn production for the RSC with Ian McKellen, Judi Dench, John Woodvine, Bob Peck, Roger Rees, David

28

Howey, Sue Dury, oh and a dozen actors who can make theatre a pleasure above and beyond all others.

The Royal Court version was not quite in the same league – that would be like comparing Donny Osmond to Pavarotti. Even though the two stars, Alec Guinness and Simone Signoret, were justly celebrated throughout the Western world for their undoubted talents, the beginnings were not auspicious. Rehearsals didn't go well. Simone was having great difficulty with the knotty Elizabethan language, hard enough for an English let alone a French actress. Sir Alec wore a natty tracksuit throughout the rehearsal period. When asked why, he remarked significantly that doing Macbeth was like running a three-mile race. Meanwhile, he was perfecting a Glaswegian accent for the part. Jack Shepherd, playing the Porter, had elected to base his character on a chicken, a brave but controversial decision, though he finally persuaded everyone to his point of view. (He later went on to become a mainstay of the National Theatre Company.) Zakes, one of the three black witches, was worrying about the racial and political overtones in the casting as only a few of the cast were really Scottish – a good point, but one that nobody had time to address properly until after the show had opened, by which time it was too late. The mighty Sue Engel had a ferocious argument with our beloved director in the bar of the theatre (this bar was later gutted by fire) about whether if a mother saw her young child being murdered by a couple of killers, she would try to go to the child's aid or run away to save her own skin. Ms Engel said she would go to her child's aid and she knew this to be right because she, unlike Bill, was a woman and knew very well how a mother would behave. Bill disagreed, arguing, as far as I could judge – that his sophisticated sensibility, refined and matured by travels along the upper highways of human experience, told him that self-preservation would be the overriding imperative and that therefore a mother would indeed run away and leave her child. When my opinion was canvassed, I instantly agreed with Bill, my employer, and Sue in turn agreed to run away, but she was not pleased. Particularly, she was not pleased with me – I could tell. It wasn't a pleasant experience, I reflected over a plate of chips (all I could afford after the previous night's bevying). I resolved not to take part in such discussions in the future but to maintain a calm, detached aloofness, all-seeing, all-knowing, all-accommodating; I also resolved to wash my socks, which, I noticed, were getting a little high.

The production was not a success – I was not mentioned, despite my valiant attempt at the third murderer. Alec's novel portrayal of the serial killer as a dyspeptic Glaswegian bank manager was greatly misunderstood by critics and audiences alike, as was Simone Signoret's softly spoken, very French portrayal of his wife. The revolutionary decision to play the whole drama in unchanging, unblinking, blazing light in what looked like the inside of a large, sand-coloured box was also decried as being contrary to the spirit of the play, which expressed itself mainly through images of darkness. Jack Shepherd's Porter was treated more kindly, though he could have done with one or two of the 'knock, knock' jokes that David Troughton inserted in a later Adrian Noble production of the play for the RSC.

Knock, Knock
Who's there?
Duncan.
Duncan who?
Duncan disorderly.

Inventive stuff indeed, which our production sadly lacked.

However, there was one minor success, even if that was by default. Alec had given each of us a very acceptable first-night gift: a bottle of White Horse whisky. Fine for most of us, but not for Dave Terris – a Welshman of note, famously flatulent and with a prodigious capacity for drink. He proceeded to demolish the bottle before curtain up and was consequently pleasantly suffused and happy, particularly throughout the first scene. He stood towards the back of the stage, as brightly lit as everywhere else, gently swaying as he held his banner and with a half-smile on his shining face. It is true that he got a little maudlin and morose during the latter part of the performance, and that the smile faded somewhat, but no matter, he had made his mark. And his fortune: a major national theatre critic wrote something like this:

> At the back of the stage as Macbeth's mighty deeds were recounted, stood a lowly but observant thane, I know not his name, but on his face was an enigmatic smile, he rocked gently back and forth as if revelling in some secret knowledge he alone possessed. This spirit of enigma was later taken up by Sir Alec, and indeed it informed the rest of the play with a fruitful ambivalence.

This, however, was the only good review we received. We were booed by the first-night audience, and I was so depressed I drank nearly all my wages and had to lie to the collector on the underground about having lost my ticket. The cast generally were dispirited and started introducing jokes and new bits into the show to liven up the proceedings. Don D. Eagle, one of the actors, brought a water pistol into the wings and fired on the Three Witches as they were performing the opening scene. They accused one another of spitting and the whole thing got unpleasantly juvenile and

31

heated. Audiences grew restive and the sides of the sand-coloured box, stretching up into the flies, began to bend and buckle audibly during performances as the bright lights sent temperatures soaring. Pine needles fell off the branches we used to create Birnham Wood; they wouldn't have concealed a wren anyway. One actor, Jack Tower, found this irresistibly funny and had to leave the stage because he couldn't speak for giggling. For some reason the audience found the appearance of a bright-green likeness of Alec's head, impaled on a very long spear, even more irresistibly funny and sometimes clapped the spectacle.

Finally, Alec, who never reads reviews, and the lovely and hurt Simone Signoret, victim of a level of stupidity unbelievable among supposedly sensitive and artistic people, left for pastures new. The production, however, continued, with Sue Engel as Lady M and Maurice Roëves as the man himself. No problem there, except that Maurice is rather small and Susan is rather tall, and a certain amount of gravitas is undoubtedly lost when the male protagonist is forced to address most of his speeches to a spot just below the lady's chest.

The whole experience was rather depressing, but it wasn't wasted. I learned from Alec Guinness how even great celebrity cannot guarantee immunity from the slings and arrows of outrageous fortune, and how that same celebrity can generate a critical silence about itself, preventing people of goodwill and good counsel from telling you that there are certain things even you shouldn't or can't do; and from Simone Signoret I learned how admirable is an unforced gentleness and generosity when it goes hand in hand with great talent.

Stuffing these few pearls of wisdom into my otherwise empty purse, I left Sloane Square and the capital for the provincial repertory companies, and played these quite happily for many a long year. Not always to large audiences it must be said. I think the smallest was four, at the Traverse Theatre in Edinburgh – and that was before the interval: we lost fifty per cent for the second half.

But what matter, the work was intrinsically worth doing. It was art, and we looked down our noses in supercilious fashion at the better attended commercial shows in other theatres which actually made money. We were in no danger of doing that.

We did, however, have a minor problem with a highly cultured play that the management had ambitiously mounted: *Women Beware Women.* The problem stemmed from the fact that the smallness of the audience was matched only by the smallness of the stage – about ten feet square. Most of the characters in the play die horrible deaths at the end, made more horrible by the fact that there was simply not enough room for all the spreadeagled bodies on the stage and no room at all for the Cardinal – a small but important character in the drama – to stand and deliver the last, very effective oration. Fanciful suggestions that we should fall on top of each other were dismissed as being undignified and, more to the point, dangerous: those who died first were small, delicate females, while those who died last were hulking great fellows who could seriously injure the ladies if they fell on them from a great height in a frenzy of histrionic passion and flying codpieces.

It was a ticklish problem, but after a short break in the bar upstairs I had a brainwave. What if the effect of the poison was not to make the victims leap up and down and then fall flat on their faces, but rather to make them curl up in a very small ball as if they had severe stomach cramps? They could then all die leaning against the upstage wall, leaving room for the Cardinal's final grand speech.

At first there was much disagreement – it was a very democratic company – but finally the director, Dougal Mac-Gordon, adopted my bold plan. It worked a treat. Even although there was hardly any audience, hardly any of them laughed and, more importantly, the Cardinal had acres of room to deliver that final speech.

Incidentally, my playing of the Cardinal was much appreciated in the local press.

I was learning all the time. I betook myself to Exeter, even though an erstwhile friend said that the best thing about the place was that it had a by-pass. I had a very happy time there, playing John Osborne's angry young man, Jimmy Porter. I lost but, undeterred, went on to play most theatres up and down the country, ending up a member of the Royal Shakespeare Company in Stratford-upon-Avon. I enjoyed my time there immensely and think it most unkind of a fellow actor of my acquaintance to refer to Stratford as Luton with gables. It is much more than that with its lovely old antique shops, amazing Shakespeare World Experience (just by McDonald's) and the impressively large Hilton Hotel with all its flags.

Stratford is a place where many an actor has come of age, particularly in those bijou cottages along the waterside. I, too, matured there. However, there was one large disappointment: try as I and several of my chums might, and though we searched the cemetery of Stratford's church diligently one night after a visit to the Sooty Cygnet, we could not find Shakespeare's tomb. I would have searched again had I returned for another season.

But it was not to be. After several interviews at the BBC, I was phoned up at eleven-thirty one Monday morning and offered the part of the Jersey detective James Bergerac. I was faced with a terrible, heartrending choice: should I go back to the classical theatre I loved, or take the lead in a cops and robbers show on TV? I desperately needed to think what I should do. I needed time: I was given time. I debated fiercely with myself. How could I weigh the relative merits of saying 'It is I, Hamlet the Dane' with 'Hello, I'm Jim Bergerac from the Bureau des Etrangers'? Could I leave that wonderful if underpaid company of stage actors beavering away in the decent obscurity of the classical theatre, for the more vulgar if better paid delights of television stardom? It was hard. Dear God, it was hard. At eleven-thirty-five I phoned through my decision.

2
The Fan

'... So may the outward shows be least themselves
The world is still deceiv'd with ornament.'
Merchant of Venice

Fans come in all shapes and sizes, and all ages from six to ninety-six. Most are calm, orderly people, possessed of enough intelligence to distinguish reality from the obvious fiction of a TV detective series in which a 1947 clapped-out Triumph can overtake with ease a gleaming new Jaguar SJ6 and in which the rather scrawny hero can dispatch with one unerring blow a six foot, sixteen stone stuntman who has in his time fought Henry Cooper.

Not too difficult to distinguish the actual from the pretend, you might think, and you would be right. But there is a lunatic fringe of fans, made up of some very peculiar people indeed who seem incapable of making such a distinction. They write to me, and to people like me, and they call me Jim and they offer me undying love, devotion and the occasional pair of knickers (all from Marks & Spencer – why is that?). They are rarely young, nubile ladies, you understand, but mature matrons with grown-up families and benign, middle-aged husbands who seem to imagine that I

37

can do amazing things for them – or more accurately that a certain James Bergerac can do amazing things for them.

He probably can, whereas I, though not naturally constrained by modesty, confess that I am usually bereft of any ideas about how to respond. I know that that great paragon of truthfulness the *News of the World* dubbed me 'heart throb' in an article under the characteristically tasteful headline 'All the Girls Want to Grasp Nettles', but I also know that in this isolated instance the reporters had somehow got it wrong. I was not, am not a heart throb.

I am also certainly not a psychiatrist. So I decided on a masterly policy of not replying to these letters, in the hope that they would stop. They didn't. There was a certain wife of Bath who wrote to me over a period of three years – long, well-written letters full of extremely intimate details of her private life. Together with the letters, she sent many photographs of herself looking variously sad and sexy, and always very beautiful. The dark-haired lady staring at me from the photographs did not look at all like my idea of the sort of person who might feel impelled to unburden her soul to a deeply unserious MC such as myself.

Why did she do it? I had no idea then and only the beginnings of one now. The ending of the affair was suitably heart-rending. She sent me a long farewell letter, some of it in verse of a very acceptable standard, stating that as I had not called her on any of the phone numbers she had given me, and as I had not replied to any of the previous 114 letters, she was forced reluctantly to conclude that I did not want to spend the rest of my life with her. To mark our parting she enclosed a tape of Ken Dodd singing 'Tears for Souvenirs'. I yield to no one in my admiration for the great Liverpudlian.

Perhaps if she had seen me as nature intended and not as

the cameraman and make-up girl designed, things would not have reached such a pretty pass. I know, to my cost, that face-to-face confrontation can swiftly disabuse a fan of many a preconceived notion. This can be a traumatic experience for the fan, because in most cases the images seen on the screen or on the stage are distorted by the medium and are at odds with the real thing. Thus actors who are thought to be hefty six-footers turn out to be tiny in real life. Paul Newman, Robert Redford, Ian Holm, Sylvester Stallone, Dolly Parton – wonderful actors all – seemed to me to be very large people; it was quite a shock to discover that they are really quite small.

I don't know why I was unprepared for people to be more than a little disappointed in my real-life appearance, but unprepared I was, and very unprepared for the good lady who turned up when I was opening a shop in Southampton. It was a public appearance much like any other: I was to appear at the shop, sit behind a table, flash the caps, sign a few autographs, exchange pleasantries with the crowd – a lucrative and usually enjoyable experience. However, this time the omens were not good. The day was dismal, fog hung about the city and my plane was late, I just had time for a rancid cup of coffee and a splash of eau-de-Cologne behind the ears before the security guards, newly employed and extremely large and keen, frog-marched me through the crowd in very close formation. (Why they had to do this, I don't know. I certainly felt in no danger of assassination.) I was deposited on a small stage on which were a chair, a table, a flask of water, two or three pens and a pile of photographs of yours truly to be signed for the good Sotonians.

The crowd moved forward and the ritual began. A young, pretty girl remarked cheekily that my photograph did me a lot of favours. It did. It had been taken some years before,

The Fan

when I had some remnant of youth clinging about my person. I remarked smoothly that maturity brings its own rewards and the session continued. Suddenly there was a pause and I looked up. There at the front of the queue stood an impressively stout lady, with a faded fawn mac, belted tightly round her ample midriff, and a plastic rain cap ringing her neck. Her sensible brown brogues were damp with rain, as were the three plastic carrier bags she was clutching. Cropped hair curled damply about her oval face and glasses glinted harshly in the bright store light. Her mouth was working feverishly, saying something that I couldn't quite catch.

I leant forward, calling for quiet so that we could all hear what she said. Perhaps, I thought, she was so overcome by seeing her hero in the flesh that she couldn't move towards me but was transfixed to the spot by awe and gratitude. I had heard of cases like this and would be kind and winsomely self-effacing when confronted by such adulation. I motioned her forwards but she waved her clanking plastic bags at me furiously. In an unmistakable gesture of refusal, her arms dropped to her sides and she gave vent to her feelings. I live on a farm and sometimes the farmer separates the mother cow from her newly born calf and leaves her tethered just outside my window. There's no malice in this, just a lack of space. And much as that distraught animal throws back its head and trumpets its distress, so did this woman.

'No, no, no. You're not like him. Not at all. It's not him at all. I've been cheated. Why do you look like that? What have they done?'

There was silence. She stood quite still, her eyes riveted to mine. With dazzling perspicacity I realized that I had completely misjudged the good lady's state of mind. I fought a rearguard action as best I could, quickly dropping my air

41

of princely modesty in favour of one of jocular *bonhomie*.

I tried: 'Well, they can do wonders with make-up.' It wasn't a very clever remark, but it was the best I could manage.

There was a short pause. 'They must do,' she said, turned on her heel and marched off.

It was all very depressing, being caught without the dressing provided by a film production team. I mean the sympathetic lighting, the supportive make-up (bringing out what remains, as one senior make-up artist remarked), the pretty background, the trendy clothes and the flash dialogue. I had been caught bare and wanting in a public place, with nowhere to hide, but at least I was recognized – after a fashion. Mercifully, I was able to call on two experiences I had had while filming at the Stokes Poges golf course some years earlier, before I became a fully-fledged MC, and they helped me endure the trauma of Southampton.

The first encounter took place in the morning, between shots. I met a kindly man. His was not a name to conjure with now, but some years before he had been famous for a cigarette advertisement. You might remember the format – our hero, depressed and lonely, wanders through an anonymous urban landscape; he takes out a packet of Strand cigarettes, lights up and immediately a look of intense pleasure suffuses his features; the catch phrase, 'You're never alone with a Strand', appears. Unfortunately, although the advertisement conferred on him the status of MC, he found work extremely difficult to come by, since the whole world identified him with loneliness and depression. He drifted, rather quickly, into an undeserved obscurity. Now, I might not live up to my TV image, but at least I was not on that road.

The second encounter at Stoke Poges concerned the amiable Patrick Mower, who was starring in that particular episode of *Bergerac*. He had been famous for a long while as a leading film, television and stage actor and I was delighted to find him perfectly approachable (some celebrities, amazing though it may seem, maintain a detached, almost Olympian aloofness, which the uninformed sometimes read as patronizing arrogance; not so with Patrick). He did me the inestimable honour of introducing me to Terry Wogan, discovered hovering by his splendid brown Roller.

'He's not famous now, but he's going to be soon,' said Patrick.

I quivered with pleasure beneath Terry's gaze, and even got to shake the great man's hand. The brief encounter over, Patrick strolled off, chatting to Cecile Paoli, the extremely pretty leading lady of the show, and I betook myself to a grassy knoll to learn some words and reflect on my sudden and pleasurable elevation to the ranks of the mighty. After about an hour, I espied the handsome star walking back towards me. He had a clever plan to make a few bob.

'How about you and I leaning on a couple of irons in front of the clubhouse. Be a good advert for the place and we could make fifty pounds each out of it.'

I was amazed at such entrepreneurial audacity and unsure that we could really make money from such an exercise, but was assured that the management of the golf club would be only too happy to have a celebrity or two photographed on the course, and that indeed they would pay for the honour.

'Lunchtime, I'll go and see the owner of this gaff and set it up for the afternoon.'

Lunchtime came and off Patrick went. He returned from his mission looking gloomy.

'What happened?' I asked.

'The prat didn't know who I was,' he replied.

Remembering such things made the assault on my ego in

Southampton a little, just a little, more bearable.

It has been borne in on me forcibly that for some fans it matters very little what the object of their affection is like in real life. The partial image that is seen on the screen can be fleshed out and filled out according to the desires of the viewer, be these desires sexual, spiritual, or even pathological. Pointless for the likes of me to rush off to the gym to make myself big and butch just because one person remarked how much smaller in real life I was than she or he imagined, when someone else will surely come along and say the exact opposite. All things to all men even an accomplished MC such as I cannot be, though in fact some of the things I have appeared to be amaze even a world-weary thespian like myself.

I remember appearing on the *Stuart Hall Radio Show* in Manchester. It was, unusually, a not very intellectual edition of the programme. I don't think either of us was on good form. He because some damnable joy-riders of Liverpool had nicked his customized car and it had been returned minus a functioning clutch, and me because I had recently broken my leg and was busy drowning my sorrows in a quantity of particularly powerful white wine. We embarked on a windily metaphysical dialogue on the nature of loss and pain – both of us being MCs, our opinions were of undoubted importance. We finished around midnight, talking of the desperate divisions in our society and the envy they generated, and how it was probably that great envy that had caused Stuart's car to be nicked. In hindsight, I must confess the conversation lacked real depth, such as you would find on the *Jimmy Young Show*, but it was certainly therapeutic, and as I staggered into the early morning Manchester air, I felt a lot better for it.

The whole affair was forgotten until a little while later I

was sitting in the red Triumph Roadster, waiting to make a grand entrance into some charity fair, when a young and extremely pretty girl approached me and, in a marked Scottish accent, said, 'I want to speak to you.' Hope springing eternal, I came out with the line 'and I'd love to speak to you' (such a line should, in an ideal world, be left to smooth, sophisticated celebrities like Gerald Harper or Simon Williams, but there it was, I had plunged in). With a fine disregard for anatomical distinction and, indeed, my finer feelings, she berated me thus (I apologize for censoring the following but you will get the gist): 'You were on that programme, weren't you, you f—. Yer one of them, aren't you? F— stuck-up lardy and we though ye were one of us f— lads.' And so on she went.

I was hugely impressed by her command of demotic Anglo-Saxon; not quite so impressed with ash from her cigarette, which she flicked casually over my carefully organized hair. I reflected quietly on the variety of human experience and how it had never once occurred to me that Detective Sergeant James Bergerac figured importantly in the class struggle.

However, fans of Bergerac, I must repeat, are generally speaking smashing folk and I count some of them I have met through the programme among my best friends. They write to me and send me gifts, for which I am very grateful indeed, and I reciprocate as best I can. They come to plays I appear in and are supportive, even if, as has happened, the play is inhuman garbage and my performance mistaken and pitiful. They are loyal, so that they still watch episodes of the series which could be retitled 'Hunt the Plot', or 'Flirtations with Literacy' and complain only mildly. For the good episodes, though, they can be more than lavish with their praise. At fêtes I open, they arrive in their hundreds and are generous to the point that there is now an account containing many thousands of pounds they have donated which will go eventually to the old and the terminally ill. I am privileged to know them.

That said, there are a few fans some celebrities could well do without, and this is particularly true of female celebrities. People of a nervous disposition may find what follows distasteful, but it is a true account of what can happen to some people who, through the medium of television, find themselves guests and intimate strangers in other people's homes.

My agent sent on to me a batch of fan letters and I was reading through them. There were the normal requests for photographs and information; two little girls, aged eight and nine, sweetly asked me to marry their aunt, who was, they said, lovely but lonely; and then I came across a very peculiar letter indeed. The writer, clearly a man, was describing his auto-erotic activities while surrounded by photographs of yours truly. Only, it appeared, he couldn't achieve a proper orgasm, but instead, at the height of sexual arousal, urinated copiously. All this was described in lurid detail.

Now, I know it is at present a good career move among thespians to declare oneself a homosexual, and indeed some of my best friends, etc., etc. But I am not one of their number, and I found the whole experience somewhat disturbing, if not to say puzzling. I had never thought of James Bergerac as the object of such bizarre fantasies. I turned back to the first of six pages, closely written in a sloping hand, to check the address (there was none) and to work my way more slowly through the letter. I then discovered that the letter had not been addressed to me at all but to a rather well-known actress of considerable talent, someone who had never to my knowledge appeared in what could be called overtly

sexy or provocative roles. The letter had clearly been forwarded to me by mistake. I was quite relieved, but at the
same time fascinated. I know that excretory functions are
used as an expression of infantile, pre-pubescent sexuality,
but this was the first adult case I had ever heard of. I made
inquiries. The actress was not pleased to get her letter back,
but I was told that she had received many such letters, and
indeed that other actresses and showbiz personalities had
received similar missives from the same source. Some had
even had parcels delivered containing trousers, underpants
and pyjamas which had been soaked in urine. I think I prefer
the M & S knickers.

3
Getting the Money

'... Put money in thy purse – put but money in thy
purse –
Fill thy purse with money.'

Othello

MCs get asked to do adverts. They are sometimes paid
enormous sums of money – sometimes as much as a year's
income for a mere two days' work. Only a few, a very few,
MCs turn down the offer of such work, and bearing in mind
the transience of celebrity, the dearth of good acting jobs
and the need to live, who is there to blame them? The reasons
why MCs (particularly from the thespian ranks) are invited
to promote various products are at least paradoxical if not
downright contradictory. The manufacturers wish to give
their product a good image, so to promote it they choose
somebody like an actor from a well-known series who also
has a good image and, what is more important, integrity –
that great plus factor everyone in advertising needs so much.
The hope is that the integrity of the actor and the affectionate
esteem in which he or she is held will make a gullible public
more likely to purchase the goodies being promoted.

Of course, integrity that can be bought in this way ceases
to be worth very much, and it often looks as if the MC is not

49

celebrating the affectionate esteem of the public but cynically exploiting it. But still the serried ranks of MCs, myself included, queue up to take the money and run. Of course, this might be an over-harsh analysis. Perhaps many of the MCs who flit across our screens really do care about the products they so skilfully promote. However, from intimate experience I know that John Nettles does not have passionately strong views on the leather settees he was advertising.

My problem with adverts centres less on inner torment as to the ethics of appearing in them and more on my complete inability to perform in this area, or so it seems to me. Perhaps I'm still unconsciously reeling from my experiences in this particular field.

I once did a coffee advert, and despite getting an enormous amount of money, I produced a performance of such woodenness, it was fit only for the forestry commission. It all started in a civilized fashion. My agent rang me and, in that deep voice reserved for jobs that will add nothing to one's artistic reputation but will make an awful lot of money (from which will be deducted a 15 per cent commission, as opposed to the usual 12 per cent), told me I had hit the jackpot. A certain well-known coffee producer wanted me to take part in a series of adverts with three other more established MCs. The money was terrific – a very nice sum for the first couple and then even more if they decided to use me again, which they seemed to think was fairly certain. The advert was to include, of course, the famous shaking of the semi-clenched fist in the air at shoulder height. (I have always thought this action had more to do with auto-eroticism than selling coffee, but perhaps that was and is intentional. In any case, what did I know?)

Off to London I popped to get my costume, and very nice it was too. The trousers were a cosy brown corduroy, redolent of that much-sought-after integrity and, of course, its attendant qualities of stability and inner strength. The shirt, open-necked and traditional, appeared above a plain-speaking, no-nonsense yellow pullover in fine wool. The shoes were a confidence-inspiring plain brown with socks to match. The whole effect was of terrific ordinariness; nothing here to frighten the horses. I felt as wholesome and as lovable as a *Blue Peter* presenter – a picture of calm in a disordered world. The houses in which we filmed were tasteful too; quietly opulent, nothing noisily ostentatious, just the sort of habitat for people whose chief topic of conversation was the coffee bean.

Other MCs in the shape of Gareth Hunt and Una Stubbs appeared in the adverts too, as did a singularly beautiful actress who had had an unfortunate experience. She had been tricked into posing topless for some photographer and the results appeared in a national newspaper. Worried that her reputation for wholesomeness had been somewhat tarnished, she felt it necessary to write to the big boss of the coffee-making concern to apologize for having so scandalized the decent world. Fortunately the great man, betraying a compassion and a sense of justice unusual in one of such lofty calling, forgave the distressed thespian and she was free to pursue her career without a stain upon her character.

The adverts were made and I was dimly aware that I had not done my best work. I could not remember my words, excellent and telling though they were, and somehow I could not, despite the years spent learning my craft in minor repertory companies, show the enthusiasm and proper love for those coffee beans before me. Into my mind came a recollection of Selina Scott on breakfast TV on one occasion at about 6.30 a.m. trying to interview a man who had made an array of chunky mugs, each one moulded into a likeness

Looked as if I detested the product

of a different member of the Royal Family. They stood in rows, shining white in the studio lights. Artistically pleasing and suitably loyal though these mug-shots were, Selina couldn't – for some reason I dare say that escaped even her – think of anything to ask and seemed to want to be somewhere else. That was the very experience I was having while making these adverts. Gareth was efficient as ever; Una delightfully and winningly understated; but I was hopeless.

I tried for an interestingly ambiguous approach, doing little apart from being there in the hope that the viewer would read into the performance that which I knew wasn't really there. This has worked for a great number of actors, and a number of great actors, but it didn't work for me. In my heart I knew I had failed. Proof positive arrived via my agent, who was very upset – for me, she said. The fact that I had lost a string of lucrative contracts, and she a great deal of commission, was neither here nor there; it was the hurt to my sensitivity and professional pride that was the tragedy of the affair. Dully, she gave me the news. They couldn't use my advert because I looked as if I despised the very product I was supposed to be promoting. They kindly offered me a reduced fee, which I gratefully accepted, skulking off to nurse my injured pride.

Who knows? Perhaps one day I'll make a comeback.

4
Breakthrough

'... How beauteous mankind is! O brave new world,
That has such people in't.'

The Tempest

There it was in letters a foot high – 'John Nettles (BBC's Bergerac)' – and a very large picture of myself (just a touch glamorized). Moreover, I was appearing in the pantomime with the great Les Dawson, doyen of professional entertainers, piano-player of note, notorious cross-dresser and the man who more than any other helped raise flatulence to an art form. He was giving his determinedly masculine performance of Nurse Ada, aided and abetted by two tons of quivering femininity in the shape of The Roly Polys. Our principal boy was that epitome of Welshness, Ruth Madoc, whose legs were – and are – the eighth and ninth wonders of the world and whose voice is in a class of its own. The canny package was completed by the legendary John Noakes ('down, Shep') and the talented Mark Curry (who later gave me a *Blue Peter* badge).

I knew in my bones I had arrived, even though one of those bones was broken, since I had foolishly fallen off my bike a few weeks earlier. However, nothing was going to stop me leaping aboard this fantastic gravy-train, packed with more MCs than you could shake a stick at. What matter my character, the evil Sheriff of Nottingham, had a crutch and a limp; so did Richard III, so too did Long John Silver. It was decided that I should play the part four parts Dick to two parts Long John, and that atop a horse – at least for my first magnificent entrance, in which I was to thunder to the centre stage and deliver a speech full of fiery anger and malediction all about fairies and then exit with great trumpeting from the orchestra.

It was like being back at the RSC; it was very like being back at the RSC. I could not fail; I could not wait. I should have thought more about the horse. It was less of a mettlesome beast and much smaller than I had imagined, and instead of gleaming black after the fashion of Dick Turpin's Black Bess, Napoleon was a warm, homely fawn colour. Moreover, he was a circus horse and would not behave according to the rules I had so assiduously learned at Cynthia Binet's academy of equine art in far-off Jersey. No matter what I did, I had no effect on the beast, and consequently Napoleon had to be led at a sedate pace on to the stage by his owner, Russ, whose ability with horses was light years ahead of his ability to wear period costume convincingly. So much for the galloping entrance. Never mind, it would all be fine – not quite as fine as I first thought, but fine enough. This was over-optimistic, to say the least. I should have known I was in trouble when I saw the hardy lads of the orchestra flinch and duck behind their song sheets as the horse, excited by the occasion in all kinds of ways, pranced menacingly towards them, Russ clinging heroically to its head.

Undeterred, I launched into my opening speech, guaranteed to thrill the audience and send them off in transports of delight, back through time to a world of princes and princesses, of wood elves and goblins, of dastardly evil at odds with the beautiful and the good. I was to be the conduit to that magic realm. Classical actor of distinction, rogue and vagabond, TV star and MC extraordinaire, this was to be my finest hour.

It was a good deal less than an hour; indeed, a good deal less than a minute. I had just completed the immortal opening couplet, 'Methinks a sprite once dwelt within this dell, I recognize the signs, I know them all too well', when the horse simply walked off the stage. Russ tried to prevent him from doing so but was hindered by his helmet, which had fallen over his face. Panic set in, for I knew that my speech contained vital information about the plot which the audience had to receive or otherwise the sophistication and the fiendish complexity of the narrative would be lost upon them. I sped through the next ten lines with the exit from the stage coming closer and closer. I tried to cling as best I could to the proscenium arch and embarked upon the explanation of my very tricky relationship with my brother's sons. The horse, with me aboard, continued into the blackness of the wings. I still had sixteen lines to go, but the audience never heard them.

As you can imagine, I was distraught and emotionally drained by the experience. John Noakes tried to comfort me, opining that no one gave a toss for the plot anyway, but I was inconsolable for several performances.

I may say here that John does, in fact, combine a terrific warm-heartedness with a great deal of worldly *savoir faire*. On the occasion of Mark's birthday, we happened to see in a wire basket outside a bric-à-brac shop in Liverpool Street an LP of Des O'Connor's greatest hits, and knowing that this would make an ideal present for the youngster, he rushed

Breakthrough

into the shop to purchase it. The price had been largely washed away by the rain, which was falling in typical Manchester fashion, but the shop keeper announced it to be 40p. John demurred, pointing out the antiquity of the record and also the extensive rain damage. I think the shopkeeper must have recognized John right away, for he didn't try and argue the toss – a bargain was immediately struck and John handed over 10p for what turned out to be a most acceptable present. A small event perhaps but one that exemplifies that mixture of sentiment and northern hard-headedness that makes John the man he is.

As the beautiful Marti Caine has remarked about the money she is paid for appearing in pantomime, 'It don't half make a difference to the mortgage.' Indeed it does. Pantomimes form a principal source of income for us MCs. So do those wonderful comedies like *No Sex in My Bed Please*, *Boeing British*, etc. No matter that many of us have never seen the inside of a theatre before. No matter that lots of us can neither sing nor dance nor do anything very much apart from turn up and wave – and sometimes not even that. And curiously, even though many of us are not even very good at the job which made us famous in the first place, the great, warm-hearted British public will applaud us just for bothering to appear. I would like to thank them on behalf of us all. Thank them for putting up with performances so wooden as to make Pinocchio look like Depardieu, so wretchedly unfunny as to make Ecclesiastes read like a Feydeau farce, and so sexist as to make *Men Only* a bible of feminism. Yes, while the posh lardy theatre lies a-bleeding, magnificent mammaries, an occasional bottom, an unending supply of double and single *entendres* about nymphomaniacs and homosexuals, errant wives and perverted vicars, from some foul-mouthed comic, ever seem to form an irresistible cocktail when thrown over the footlights at an adoring public. 'Twas ever thus, if Shakespeare is to be believed, and quite rightly so. Which of us, if truth be told, has not thrown up a sweaty nightcap or two and brayed a beery celebration of our native, vulgar, Chaucerian humour. Let the French sneer, the Americans gaze in disbelief. Come all the world to mock, it is ours and ours alone. It may be rubbish, but it is British rubbish.

Mind you, it is not all plain-sailing. One must certainly be prepared to sacrifice a little pride doing pantomime. It helps to develop a thick skin quite quickly, particularly if you are an émigré from the respectable theatre and unused to the rough house atmosphere of the pantomime, which is, among other things, a theatre of insult. Now, I expect those masters of witty repartee, like Hope and Keene and John Sessions, can give as good as they get, but I must confess I was a little offended and upset and incapable of riposte when, during my first pantomime and my first encounter with Les Dawson's Dame, he turned to me and said, just because I was a little late with my entrance, 'Nettles, you are to acting what Julie Andrews is to Deep Throat.'

A hearty laugh greeted this sally, followed by a round of applause. Instead of a quiet appreciation for my outstanding characterization, the audience was laughing at me – not with me, but *at* me. I had to get my own back, but my attempts were doomed to failure, it seemed, and were greeted with a stony silence. I tried calling him an amorphic androgyne, a dead elm, a truncated transvestite, a rubicund roisterer, a turgid tergiversator, but nothing worked; my forays into alliterative wit were not successful. But Les himself came to my rescue. At that time he had just taken over from Terry Wogan as the host of *Blankety Blank*, a quiz game for intellectuals. 'Why don't you,' said the kindly comic, at the end of the scene, 'turn to me and say, "Get off, you poor man's Terry Wogan"?'

'That's feeble,' I replied, not understanding that in popular entertainment, topicality is in itself funny to an audience, and when there is a reference to a popular TV show in the gag, the fun quotient is doubled (that is why Les Dawson got a good laugh when he referred to me as that Detective Beaujolais from Sark). Reluctantly I agreed to use the great man's put-down of himself during the next show. There was a second's silence, then hysterical uproar, followed by a thunderous round of applause. Having spent all my professional life taking the credit for delivering other people's lines, I was not slow to do so on this occasion. I took a bow and learned a lesson.

It must be admitted that Les Dawson is always, irritatingly enough, very knowledgeable about what will and will not work in panto. He's also very kind in odd ways to his fellow artists. Once in Southampton, the rotund comic, in the guise of Nurse Ada, was supposedly asleep upstage while two young comics went through a lengthy routine downstage. Things weren't going too well; in fact, they were going very badly. One gag after another hit the ground with a resounding thud and the two comics, unnerved, became more manic than humorous. The silence of the audience grew in intensity. Suddenly, the atmosphere, more redolent of a Greek tragedy than a comic turn, was cleft in twain by great farting sounds from Nurse Ada's bed, followed by an order to 'get off'.

'What are you saying that for?' cried one of the hapless comics unwisely.

Dawson sat up, smiled benignly and then sang, 'Do You Think I Would Leave You Dying?' The comics departed quietly.

Les Dawson

Another wonderful sign that I had indeed arrived as an MC was when invitations to judge all manner of shows and competitions began to flow in. I know little about dried-flower arranging, but there I was, judging a dried-flower arranging contest. I know even less about dogs, but I was invited to judge a dog show – and promptly chose the dogs with the prettiest handlers, which caused no little complaint.

A lifetime's gallant failure with women had made it clear even to me that I know less than nothing about the fair sex, but I was invited none the less to judge quite a few beauty contests. One to choose Miss Grouville, here in Jersey, I shall pass over quickly as, first, nobody knew who I was, the competition being held in one of the eastern parishes where they don't have much TV, and second, none of the girls seemed very enthusiastic. One dark-haired beauty paraded on the crudely erected stage by the side of the harbour was asked by a giggling compère why she'd entered the competition. She replied that she was working as a waitress in a local restaurant and a chap had walked in five minutes before, given her a fiver and told her to get on stage to make up the numbers; she ended by asking if she could go now please, as the boss would be getting annoyed.

But then I was asked to be a judge in the Miss UK contest, to be held at the prestigious Waldorf Hotel in London and televised. This meant that my mum could see it and so witness my coming of age in the world of the MC. To please her, and also to please myself – for although, as I say, I have been a perennial failure with women, I've always loved them inordinately in every aspect – I accepted the invitation with alacrity. I duly arrived at the hotel, which is just along from the Aldwych Theatre, where I had appeared in some splendid plays with some very splendid actors in my previous incarnation as a classical actor. The contrast with my present

63

role could hardly have been more extreme. It was an exciting event, however, and organizing it was very complicated and arduous. Television technicians were swarming all over the place, fixing lights, manoeuvring cameras, putting up bits of scenery, pushing potted plants into corners; musicians snatched rehearsals where and when they could; friends and relations, lovers and agents of the beauty queens stood around, eyes everywhere, pretending to chat; and occasionally one of the actual contestants could be seen, dressed in the standard concealing and somewhat unforgiving day-glo tracksuit. There was the late and great Ray Moore, rehearsing his spiel, and there too, be still my beating heart, was the lustrous Jan Leeming, who was to conduct intimate chatettes before millions of viewers with the beauties after their appearance on the catwalk. It was all hugely exciting.

I discovered the make-up lady who was assigned to the panel of judges was none other than the exquisite Nicky, who had done a stint on *Bergerac*, so we had a good gossip about who was having whom and if they were enjoying it, who was in and who was out, and whether she could perform very much more than a holding operation on my face. She also let me in on some of the more intimate gossip about creative make-up in the beauty contest game. I was quite amazed. I had no idea so many people shoved so much down their trousers or up their jumpers to enlarge on nature's already ample gifts. Surely that sort of thing did not go on in a respectable show like Miss UK. Surely nowadays beauty shows were not about crass sexuality, with women paraded for the dubious delight of greasy voyeurs. Surely nowadays cool, artistic judgements were made about aesthetically pleasing forms and, above all, the engaging personalities of the contestants. These were the important considerations, not whether the women aroused libidinous thoughts unfit

64

for the decent light of day. And yes, indeed, this was the case. I knew it to be so because the organizer of the show told me in as many words: 'We don't want any smut or anything like that,' he confided to us judges, screwing up his face the better to convey his distaste, nay disgust, at the very idea of smut creeping into his wholesome exhibition.

He was a small, stocky man, with an accent like Wilfred Pickles, red of face and very proprietorial and caring about his show. There were certain rules to be obeyed. After the swimsuit section, which would be recorded for inclusion in that night's show, he told us in conspiratorial tones that we were to 'interview' the girls one by one in a small room upstairs. There was to be no smut, you know, no suggestive remarks or anything, and to make it absolutely fair, we were not to be allowed to ask the individual girls whatever we liked. Indeed, we couldn't ask them any questions at all. No, they were going to be asked the same questions by the Northern Man himself and we could listen to their replies and make our judgements accordingly.

We went to our places to observe the swimsuit parade. The girls appeared one by one in extraordinary costumes, cut just beneath the armpit. Now, dear reader, I did try very hard to banish all 'smutty' thoughts, but it was exceedingly difficult, and had I not been assured to the contrary, I would have mistakenly thought that arousal was the name of the game. I found myself feeling guilty and sweating profusely, but I put it down to being brought up in the 1950s and the hot television lights. Acres of lightly tanned, gently undulating flesh caressed my eyeballs; honed muscle swelled magnificently and provocatively along the endless thighs; perfectly formed breasts, hard-nippled, thrust through the gossamer thin and yielding silk; bottoms rose, tensed and fell like gentle waves on a summer sea; mouths were wet, half-open and, if Nicky's gossip were not true, God had blessed these girls beyond the dreams of Venus.

This dazzling and disturbing display over, my fellow judges and I rushed up to the aforementioned small room where the so-called interviews were to take place. It was dingy to start with and seemed even more so after the glare of the television lights. There was a long table, behind which we sat, our backs to the window. Four chairs were positioned to the right of the table and at an angle to it, so they were facing into the centre, where a single chair was waiting for the contestants. Our mentor gave us some more timely advice about avoiding smut and any form of suggestiveness, then he and his wife sat down on the chairs by the table. In front of us were printed copies of the questions the girls were to be asked.

Since time immemorial, and certainly since the time of Socrates, who perfected the art, the inquisitorial question and answer approach has produced startling results in every field of human endeavour. Ask the right question and you are well on the way to getting the information you require. Ask the wrong question, however, and you may be lost for ever. Every detective and scientist in the world knows this to be true. Apparently our man did not. With the best will in the world, I could not see how questions of such awesome fatuity as 'Where would you like to go on holiday?' or 'What do you think of Prince Charles's love life?' would elicit answers of a sort to enable us judges to make a proper assessment of the contestants' intellect and personality. Further difficulty presented itself when we realized that they were still in their bathing suits. As the first one walked in, our friend introduced her by saying, 'And here, ladies and gentlemen, is Miss X, who almost got into her costume.' This was obviously an OK non-smutty remark, for he laughed uproariously; his wife allowed herself a tight smile.

It is very difficult when you are dressed in a black jacket and bow tie to interview a half-naked young lady you have never met before. It must be difficult for her too, particularly when her so-called inquisitors hardly speak and are silhouetted against a window so she can't see their faces clearly. It is even more difficult if you have to answer questions of such mind-bending idiocy as to make the head ache intensely. But they tried. Oh, how they tried. Most of them were extremely nervous. One beautiful and understandably inarticulate girl was almost crying in her efforts to respond intelligently, and trembling like a young doe that has just been savaged by a pack of Rottweilers. Her haunches rigid, her knuckles white, she gripped the edge of the chair, her exposed flesh crawling with goose pimples.

I was becoming more than a little disillusioned with the whole proceedings, but I sat through the live section of the contest in which the girls, who must have been desperately tired by this time, disported themselves for our delectation and appraisal. I kept hoping a group of feminists would appear and destroy the spiritually threadbare spectacle. The show went on. Some other MC whose name I can't remember chatted briefly to each of the contestants – I don't know what his first language was. We handed in our papers and the winner, to whom I had given all the marks at my disposal in the sure knowledge that this would ensure her victory, was given that final accolade, being interviewed by a famous newsreader. And then it was over. Dinner was served in the cellars of the hotel. I tried to get a little chat with the winner but she was whisked away by some large gentleman. It was getting late. I felt unaccountably depressed and went to my very big bed in my very small room.

The next day I had two radio interviews, the first with

Tony Blackburn. I wasn't really up to it. He asked me difficult questions such as was I frightened of being typecast and, even more awkwardly, did I like Jersey? Somehow I survived this gruelling encounter and rushed round to Capital Radio, to be quizzed by the famous and amiable Michael Aspel. As it was fresh in my mind, I started talking animatedly about the beauty contest, describing it among other things as a flesh market, a demeaning and dispiriting experience for all the participants, the last gasp of an outdated, discredited and inhuman philosophy of sexuality which should be extinguished utterly and entirely once and for all. Michael bore all this with laudable equanimity but looked, I thought, just a little pale, maybe even cross. Could that be true? Half-way through my tirade, I realized, of course too late, that Michael Aspel had famously compèred more beauty contests than I'd had good parts. It was with no little relief, and a very large vodka, that I returned to my island retreat.

5
The Cost of It

'... There is so great a fever on goodness that the dissolution of it must cure it. Novelty is only in request.'
Measure for Measure

Some little time ago, before *Bergerac* became a programme about wine-producing and was about a Jersey police officer, I had the great good fortune to be cast with several rather beautiful actresses, who were, without a single exception, a delight to work with. These lovely creatures rescued many a dull script from a richly deserved oblivion. Most beautiful amongst the beautiful was Lisa Goddard, an actress of enormous charm and vivacity with a rather formidable intellect who, when she was not appearing with that epitome of MCdom Lionel Blair, would pop across to Jersey to enchant the dull Jersey cop.

Reality came not far behind the fiction in that I always felt a little lumpen when she was around – two green shield stamps short of a toaster, so to speak. Despite this the lovely lady befriended me and my daughter, who took Lisa as a role model. (It was a little difficult having two Lisa Goddards around the place, but I managed somehow.) I was introduced to her husband, the inimitable Alvin Stardust, and to their

69

two children – as attractive as their parents. We became friends, all of us, as people do – or rather, as people don't.

I had not realized, of course, that MCs are not allowed friends, and certainly not friends of the opposite sex. They are expected to have, and indeed do have, lovers. Proof positive that myself and Lisa were a rather mature version of Romeo and Juliet lay in the fact that we WERE SEEN TOGETHER AT A RESTAURANT, and leaving my HOUSE, and sitting TOGETHER on a beach while my GIRLFRIEND sat some YARDS AWAY obviously UPSET! Anxious to know how my private life was progressing, I gave up rereading my old reviews and hungrily gathered to me all tabloids, weekdays and Sundays. All was wonderful, I learned. My girlfriend had now become my ex-girlfriend (I rang her with the news. She was as excited as I was to know more about what we were doing.)

The TV love affair had become a real-life love affair – a passionate and torrid love affair indeed, in which Lisa had left her husband for me and had moved into my house, even though it was a humble abode and not at all what she was used to (further indication of intensity of passion). Photographs appeared of us in passionate embraces – I could have sworn they were stills from a *Bergerac* episode, but I was obviously mistaken, for there was no mention of this in the accompanying text. The opinions of 'insiders' and 'close friends' had thoughtfully been sought, so as to keep readers properly informed. These insiders and close friends all agreed to our deep and abiding love for each other. Others of my friends, however, had stupidly and irresponsibly tried to stop this gathering together of vital information by refusing the £5,000 offered for my telephone number and details of my private life. Had I been in their position, I would not have refused, for I know that such action is futile, having been

The Cost of It.

told so some years before by a perfumed purveyor of truth from the *Daily Mirror* who remarked that even if I did not grant him an interview, he would nevertheless get the information he required by recourse to the 'hit squad'. I wonder what that could have been.

So there it was. High summer, Jersey, and I was having a wonderful adulterous affair with a very glamorous lady. What could be more pleasant for me, my daughter and my girlfriend, for Alvin Stardust, Lisa Goddard and for their two children? While reflecting on these momentous events in my life – I was filming on a boiling hot day up at the airport, being very forceful with even more stuntmen – I got a phone call from our parish sergeant, Gerry McFarland, who, despite his name, is as Jersey as they come and as fine an officer as you could wish to meet. Apparently my house was besieged by reporters and photographers and neither Lisa nor my daughter, who didn't wish to see them, could get out. What did I want him to do about it? Being in real life possessed of a Hamlet-like indecision, I did not have the faintest idea, but fortunately the good policeman did, and with a cheery 'Leave it all to me', he put the phone down.

My performance that afternoon was even more unsmiling and dour than usual, for I was anxious that no harm should befall these brave and good people from the cutting edge of investigative journalism. I had heard tales of Jerseymen's treatment of strangers before, and none of them was pleasant. I mean, these people had in the past cut Huguenot throats, viciously attacked Guernseymen for no reason other than that they were Guernseymen, and even, it is said, pushed an Italian over a cliff for betraying a Todt worker to the Germans. God alone knew what they might do to members of an alien fourth estate.

I need not have worried. The good sergeant with commendable expedition and, as we shall see, even more commendable intention, leapt into a police car with a junior colleague and arrived hot-foot at the theatre of creative newsgathering. Sergeant Gerry introduced his colleague to the panting newshounds as having something of import to impart to them. Now, PC David McAllister really is a Scot and his accent, with respect, is very broad. In fact, it is impenetrable to anyone born much beyond Glasgow – and even for many born within that fair city's limits. As far as the glowing hacks could make out, John and Lisa were 'Nay more in the hoose' but were camped up at a place called Grève de Lecq, in the far, far north of the island and thither would he lead them in furious convoy to conduct interviews and click away to their hearts' content. Thither, indeed, the stalwart constable led them, while Lisa and my daughter made good their escape. And there he left them, in the rather large car park, saying Nettles and Goddard would appear later. They were bereft of transport and, more sadly, bereft of any knowledge as to where they were. Now, Jersey is only nine miles by five, but you'd be surprised how extraordinarily easy it is to get lost. One theory is that the islanders took down all the sign-posts to hinder the Germans, and just forgot to put them up again after the war. Be that as it may, the scandalous pair did not turn up that entire afternoon and I would hazard a guess that the Fleet Street boys were not best pleased.

Some three or four weeks later I was still, according to my trusty tabloids, having a wonderful time with the delectable Ms G. But then things apparently began to go seriously wrong. Suddenly I was not having an affair at all. Ms Goddard, far from rejoicing in the publicity afforded the new love in her life, was actually denying there was one at all. I was mortified, and went into a swift decline. How could that possibly be true, thought I, gazing morosely into a large glass of warm Bell's, when the *News of the World* had positively stated otherwise? I had to take steps to find out the truth, but it came unbidden in the shape of a newspaper article headlined: LISA GETS LIBEL DAMAGES. I gasped in astonishment at what followed. We were not having, nor ever had had, an affair; we were, of all things, just good friends. My world collapsed in micro seconds. Further 'substantial damages' had been paid to Ms Goddard by the *News of the World* for printing such a story. I felt cheated and desolate and took at least a fortnight to recover my usual equanimity. If this is what it was like to be an MC, I wanted none of it. Here one minute, gone the next. I mean, people getting paid for not having affairs with me.

6
Come on Down

Among the many glittering prizes dangled before the rising MC is that prize of prizes, the chance to appear on the celebrity quiz or chat show – the quintessential, intellectual quest, conducted by inquisitors with curious coiffures. Why do the presenters of these shows have such a predilection for the bizarre when it comes to hairstyles?

Now, I wear a wig, but I introduced it gradually, so that my legion of fans, who will have no truck with the ageing process, would not be suddenly shocked by the appearance of a luxurious growth of hair of doubtful colour in all kinds of new places. Following the advice of my friend and mentor Terence Alexander, I diplomatically and surreptitiously applied (small) quantities of burnt cork to those areas of scalp showing beneath the thinning hair. As these areas increased in size, I gently, secretively, unobtrusively introduced small and then larger hair pieces, and I shall continue to do so. It is true that what with bridge work, contact lenses and the aforementioned toupees (I have two, an indoor one and an outdoor version of more robust design, the better to withstand the Jersey squalls), I leave more in the bathroom than I take to bed, but I regard this as part of the price of being such a famous person.

The essence of disguise is gradualism. You must introduce the changes needed to make you look the same slowly, so people don't notice. It is no use appearing one minute as wobbly and multi-chinned as Robert Morley or Ian Carmichael, and the very next as firm and lantern-jawed as Cliff Richard or Simon Williams, for people will notice, just as they will notice if one day you are smooth and bald as an ostrich egg and the next, as hirsute as an orang-utan. You cannot pull the wool over the eyes of the great British public, and it was absolutely pointless our famous quiz master turning up at the studio with a full head of straw-coloured hair, when he had been spotted the day before without any. If it had grown in the space of one night, then not since Lazarus has there been such a revival and the miracle should have been duly recorded and our amiable host duly canonized. If, as a few of us think, it was not the work of God but that of a certain well-known and discreet establishment a little to the east of Park Lane, then the whole exercise was futile, lacking that touch of essential subtlety which might have ensured its success.

Strangely, I have not been asked on many quiz or chat shows, perhaps because I hadn't got a book to flog, fashioned coffee mugs in the shapes of the Royal Family, recently made a movie with Bob Hoskins, had a chat show of my own or recorded anything in the 1960s. I do not count Les Dawson's invitation to appear on *Blankety Blank*, as that was not really a quiz show at all but an excuse for the great man to settle old scores by verbally mugging the guests. (Terence Alexander, against my advice, did appear on that programme, but on his own admission found the rules so difficult that he couldn't understand them and therefore didn't have a very pleasant time. I forbore to make capital from his discomfiture.)

I put this dearth of invitations down to word getting out concerning my unfortunate showing in a venerable, not to say venerated, quiz show *Call My Bluff*. In case anyone does not know it, the idea of the programme is exquisitely simple, like most good ideas. Definitions of an obscure word are given by individual members of one team of three to the opposing team and they have to decide if the definition is true or bluff. What could be simpler? Like those great thespians Roy Marsden (who bravely doesn't wear a toupee in real life) and Dennis Waterman (ditto) before me, I would employ my undoubted talents to good effect in such a forum. Or so I felt, but I was horribly mistaken. Though I flattered myself I was pretty damn good at the more abstruse classical roles and could make a decent attempt at TV acting, the proper way to behave on a quiz show defeated me almost completely. Not that people didn't try to help me. Frank Muir told me that I should smile a lot as I had a nice smile. I decided to follow his advice. Robert Robinson was suitably encouraging. The director told me that dress was informal above the waist and no one could give a monkey's about what went on below. So was it all right if I chose to wear directoire knickers and an open-necked shirt? I asked in jocular fashion. But he had already departed to see if the beauteous Rula Lenska was anywhere near ready.

There were two editions recorded back to back and I remember little about either except that I smiled a lot during the first one but was told to stop smiling for the second. No reason was vouchsafed me. I also remember being fascinated by Robert Robinson's profile, having never seen the great man from this angle before. From where I was sitting, I could

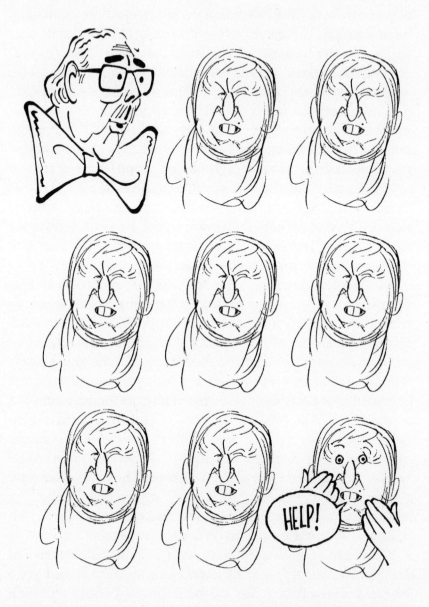

Frank Muir told me I should smile a lot.

observe in detail the byzantine complexity of the coiffure. I hope I am not betraying any secrets when I say that the hair which appears lying serenely athwart the upper dome of that distinguished skull has its origins in the nape of the neck, whence it is swept boldly upwards and across like a curlicue in a work by Aubrey Beardsley cunningly to suggest, no more than that, real growth on top of the head. The whole effect is breathtaking, and I have it on higher authority than my own that the tension between the sophisticated artifice of the hairdo and the contrasting unforced naturalness of Robert's discourse 'is the reason for his enduring appeal. Perhaps it was because I was distracted by such sights and thoughts that I again failed to take advantage of the opportunities offered me as an MC.

I sat back with a glass of Krug (chilled) and a few chums with glasses similarly charged to view the show as it was transmitted. It was a gloomy experience. I had clearly taken Frank's advice much too much to heart and, in fact, never stopped smiling for the entire first show. But it wasn't really smiling as we know it in the sense of an unforced and relaxed expression of pleasure. It was more akin to the grimacing of a prize mare who sees Christopher Timothy wandering in close proximity, putting on a rubber glove. Small comfort in the fact that our side won. The second show was even worse, if that were possible. I did not smile at all during this. Indeed, my expression would have suited Macbeth *in extremis* in Act V, sc. vii, first two lines. No comfort at all this time. I lost the game utterly for my team.

There is a curious tailpiece to this story, demonstrative of how really sensitive some viewers can be. Weeks had gone by since the transmission of the show and I was enjoying myself hugely having what I thought of as a well-earned break at my home near Stratford-upon-Avon, which, as I've said already, is not quite the Luton with gables one well-known actor called it but something far greater. I'm sorry if this offends some of my more purist thespian chums, but I believe there is no greater place to be than sitting in the Swan or the Memorial Theatre, watching the country's best actors performing Shakespeare well (of course, there are times when they perform it bloody awfully, but that is invariably the director's fault). Anyway, there I was, resting, in the land of the Bard, well out of the glare of publicity, my experience on *Call My Bluff* mercifully receding, when I received two letters, forwarded to me by my agent. I took them to be straightforward fan letters, but was quickly disabused of this notion. The first was from a retired major, who took me severely to task for appearing improperly dressed on the programme.

> You might think appearing without a tie clever. It is no such thing. I quite liked you in your own programme, you seemed quite a decent chap, but I am very disappointed to see you appear so casually and sloppily dressed on *Call My Bluff*. I suppose you think of it as style. Let me assure you it is no such thing. It is merely distasteful.

Strong words indeed, but worse was to come in the second letter, which was even more outspoken, though the writer had not, as far as I could judge, experienced the inestimable civilizing influence of army life. It was oozing bilious complaint, the burden of which was that by appearing without a tie in an open-necked shirt I had failed to 'show any reverence or respect for [my] elders and betters on the programme' (presumably Robert Robinson, Dennis Quilley, Frank Muir, Rula Lenska *et al.*), and that I had done irreparable harm to those conventions of civilized behaviour which alone stood between us and barbarism and wasn't I ashamed of myself. Of course I was. The brute force of his logic hit home. I tore the letter up in the manner of the person he said I was, and sent it back to him, minus a stamp. The missive from the Major I hung in the loo.

My appearance on a Christmas edition of *A Question of Sport* was an altogether different experience. The pungent smell of formaldehyde didn't hang so obviously about the studio. Everyone seemed jolly and relaxed. All the men were wearing open-necked shirts. What matter if by the time I arrived for the recording of the third show that day the few remaining sandwiches were curled up like Chinese crackers and the white wine had turned to vinegar, for I was with some of the greatest luminaries of the sporting world. Bill Beaumont, the ex-rugby player, was there, a very large gentleman who perpetually smiles but only faintly, so that his smile is just distinguishable from a sneer. Then there was Emlyn Hughes, a counter-tenor and ex-Liverpool foot-baller of note, who on occasions makes hilarious and irre-sistible comedy from the funny-sounding names of foreign footballers. The truly great England captain Bryan Robson was there too, having just appeared on the previous programme. I tried to impress him with how I had broken my leg, but since he had broken nearly every bone in his body, and often more than once, my story fell a little flat. There was an assortment of extremely pretty ladies there too, but I never did find out why. Ray Brooks, the actor and the voice of a thousand ads was there, appearing in Emlyn's team, as was Stan Boardman; and Little, from that dynamic comic duo Little and Large, was there because he was appearing with me in Bill Beaumont's team. David Coleman was, of course, the chairman in a very natty jumper indeed.

Now, putting me in a sports quiz show is rather akin to

81

entering a Lada in a Formula One motor race – brave but stupid. My sporting days and interest in sport effectively ended when I left school at eighteen. That I had been school First XI captain was more to do with seniority, sobriety and an ability to write out the team selections legibly than any perceptible footballing skills I possessed. Fortunately, because it was a Christmas show, I managed to get a squint at some of the questions that would be asked me directly. I must confess at first that I more than o'erstepped the modesty of nature in pretending I hadn't known them, but with those great examples of professional calm before me, I soon caught the tone of nonchalant ease which is the hallmark of the programme. I did come a cropper, however, when I inadvertently revealed my abysmal ignorance of matters sporting when I mistook Harvey Smith riding a horse over a jump for Sebastian Coe. Our team captain had a definite sneer on his face, not a faint smile, as he turned to remonstrate with me. My unutterable shame was quickly forgotten as Stan Boardman replied to the next question, 'Who rode Shergar in the 1983 Derby?' with, 'I wish I knew who's bloody riding him now.'

The show over, I crept back to the theatre just down the road, where we were doing a technical rehearsal of the pantomime preparatory to opening in two days' time. There was a note on my dressing-room table saying I had been voted BBC Personality of the Year by the Variety Club of Great Britain. Now, you will find this exceedingly strange, but it is none the less true that I have received shamefully few awards over the years. In fact, I have received hardly any. I came second in the Bird and Tree competitions at school in 1956 and 1957, and was Sony's Radio Actor of the Year in 1982 – not that I actually received that award, because the telephone link from the Hilton Hotel to Jersey had been cut off in mid-conversation with the presenter and a Royal person who was to do the honours. So I was really rather pleased to be getting this award. I was even more delighted when I saw that the presenter at the award ceremony, to be held at the Hilton Hotel, Park Lane, was to be my old friend from Stoke Poges, Terry Wogan – small world for us celebrities. A glass of wine was called for.

7
Getting on Up

Yes, yes, and at last I was to receive a great accolade. I would have several glasses of wine. I phoned my agent out of office hours, usually a somewhat risky undertaking, but she immediately understood the need to share my great joy with my nearest and dearest. She rejoiced with me in my hour of triumph but sounded a note of caution, well several notes actually. The presentation ceremony at the Hilton Hotel was to be televised so it was absolutely imperative, she told me, that I looked my best and not as if I had been up half the night in the Shaftesbury with a bottle and a gang of jolly inebriates. I knew exactly what she meant, but to make absolutely sure I did not fall foul of the rules of such a great occasion and make a complete fool of myself, the great lady actually condescended to accompany me to the feast of self congratulation on the prescribed day. I was duly grateful.

I could not sleep that night for dreaming of my new glory and what I would say on accepting the fabulous prize. No, I would not do the usual thing and publicly thank a lot of people no one had ever heard of for my success. On the contrary, I would devise something novel, pithy and witty, sparkling and memorable with which to astound and amaze the glittering audience at The Hilton and also, and more importantly, those millions of people out there in television land who would doubtless be glued to the screen, in eager anticipation of seeing their hero, suave, in control, articulate as ever. I would take no chances, no chances at all. I reined in my delight. I would be extra careful for I know that there can be many a slip between the bar and the hotel bedroom. Between the intention and the act falls the shadow, or as in a famous and salutary case I remembered – the toad. It is worth repeating this story, for I have found it strangely evocative of the human condition through the ages. A sobering tale it is too, and it is significant that it came to mind on this the eve of my greatest triumph.

Leonie was a beautiful dancer, with long legs, supple body, blond hair and laughing blue eyes, not a little unlike those of Barbara Gillespie, fondly remembered from childhood days. I first saw her by St Brelades church, one glorious summer morning, staring out to sea, the sun shining through her cotton dress. My initial attempts to wheedle my way into her affections she bore with quiet good humour. She was not impressed when I told her I was an actor. She never watched television and had never heard of *Bergerac,* but she agreed nevertheless to have a cup of tea with me in the little cafe along the bay. We walked slowly along the busy seafront. I was dying for just one person, *any* person, to ask for an autograph so she would be suitably impressed at my fame. If your MC is lying crushed and bleeding in a gutter in Tangier and is in desperate need of medical attention, someone will ask for an autograph. If your MC is burying his dearest family relative, it is ten to one someone will ask for an autograph. I know this to be true. But when you actually *need* someone to ask for your autograph, where are they? They were certainly not in St Brelades bay that lusty morning.

Leonie was appearing in a local cabaret. I betook myself to see her. I saw quite a lot of her as a matter of fact, particularly during the *Sur la Plage* medley, and in the weeks that followed we tasted the delights of Jersey. I took her to my favourite restaurant, the Seacrest. The waiters there are an unruly bunch but good hearted enough and forbore to indulge in their usual ruderies when we went in. Indeed one of them addressed me as 'Sir', which I thought was over-doing it just a fraction. Anyway, I decided that if this was not love, it was something very akin. I would invite her back to my cliff top maison for a glass of Moët and an agreeable if small collation of my own invention. The invitation was made and accepted. Sunday night was the appointed time.

My friend Sean with whom I shared the house, very kindly agreed to go out for the night and leave us in peace. I believe, though I am not certain, that he was going through one of his recurrent spiritual phases and at that time took great delight in going for very long walks along the cliff tops, a slim volume of verse tucked in the back pocket. Be that as it may, I carefully prepared for Leonie. I left the front door ajar, the light beaming overhead, just to make her feel welcome. Carpets were hoovered, twice, the ashtrays emptied, the dirty clothes thrust far out of sight into the airing cupboard. The two bottles of Moët I had purchased that morning from Tescos, had been a bit warm, so I had tucked them away in the deep freeze to cool a little. Every-thing was prepared, the salad, cold meats in clingfilm, the telephone off the hook. There was an hour before Leonie was due to arrive, a small brandy to calm the nerves but not so large as to dull the senses, a delicate distinction.

I gazed through the window, the ferry, all lit up, was sailing majestically around the point, I could hear the toads, or crapauds as they are called in Jersey, croaking by the pond, and in the twilight I could just distinguish the silhouettes of dozens of rabbits sitting out for their evening feed. I may have been past the first flush of youth and deep into the long blush of middle age, but it still felt good to be alive. The minutes dragged by. The sunset glow in the skies over Guernsey began to dim toward night. Suddenly, I saw the headlights flash by the lovely Gladys, my housekeeper's house at the end of the lane. They swept up the narrow drive towards me. I decided to delay my rush to the front door until she had actually rung the front doorbell just to show how laid back and nonchalant I was. It was a short-lived decision. As she alighted from her car in a very fetching ra-ra skirt, I was standing quite manfully framed in the front doorway. I kissed her lightly on the cheek as she passed, caught the smell of expensive scent and performed a mock bow to usher her into my castle. I paused by the door to admire her as she undulated into a strangely tidy living room, turned the porch light off and took one last look around outside to make doubly sure that Sean hadn't suddenly come back. Then I went to close the stout front door. Only it would not close. Must be warped I thought, what with all that sun. I swore silently to myself, precious seconds were being wasted. The lovely Leonie was alone. Time was passing inexorably by. I took a deep breath and charged at the door with my shoulder. It hurt a lot but the door still wouldn't quite close. Nothing for it but on with the light to investigate the mystery of the intransigent portal. There was no mystery, just an appalling accident. One of the toads had crawled up between the open door and the door frame. As

88

the door was slammed so the poor fellow was crushed, but not to death I observed in horror. It was still moving. It was still alive. What could I do? I called out to Leonie in a strangely high voice that I just had to put my car away and I would not be two ticks. I unstuck the wretched crapaud from the woodwork and placed him with as much delicacy and tenderness as was humanly possible in front of my car wheel. I then drove the car straight over it twice just to make sure his suffering was at an end. I turned the engine off and sat there for some seconds, hands clammy, shaking with paroxysms of remorse. At length I gathered courage enough to go back inside to Leonie, but the evening was, in truth, ruined for me, I had been unmanned by a toad. 'You look terribly pale,' said the beautiful Leonie in a concerned tone. 'Just too much work I guess,' responded I. 'Let's have some bubbly.' As I turned towards the kitchen, there was a tremendous bang followed quickly by another. The two bottles of champagne had exploded in the deepfreeze.

It was a tragedy. I felt a little poorly, Leonie suddenly developed a searing headache, whatever was intended to be was not to be that evening. We parted half an hour later.

It was a miserable experience and taught me not to be overconfident as I gimbled along ambition's halls to the podium of achievement, located in the Hilton Hotel, Park Lane, home of brilliant smiles and warm handshakes.

I decided to travel down to London the night before the presentation ceremony which was to be held in the morning. In that way I could get a good night's sleep and have oodles of time to prepare myself calmly and properly for the ordeal ahead. I phoned my friend Beaky Mathews, residing at the time with his girlfriend, in her flat in Kensington. My luck was in. Beaky himself was out, but the girlfriend Vera answered my call. Now she is a lady of very great breeding and of a class just bordering the aristocratic and it is always and ever a pleasure to listen to her cultured voice. Yes, she breathed, absolutely fine and super if I wanted to stay the night. She looked forward ever so to seeing me but at that moment had to rush to get her young son Jeremy off to school, so far so good.

The express for London left Wilmslow where I was staying around seven o'clock in the evening. Truth to tell I was not sorry to have a break from Wilmslow, which is so exclusive it's rumoured that even the Ambulance Service is ex-directory, but for all that it is not as safe as it should be – it was from outside his house in Wilmslow that the great Stuart Hall had his customized car nicked by rapacious marauders. It was good to arrive, albeit a bit cold and hungry, in London a couple of hours later. I grabbed a taxi and headed off towards Vera's flat in Kensington. It was much smaller than expected. I had fondly assumed that all upmarket Kensington was composed of sumptuous apartments and spacious houses. Not a bit of it. Vera's flat was like nothing so much as a converted hallway, comprising a small bedroom in the front for Beaky and Vera, a tiny kitchen come living area in the centre, a bathroom and a minuscule bedroom for her son at the very end, all joined by a narrow corridor running its whole length. There was not, it appeared, a separate bedroom for me at all but there was a settee in the living area and this was to be my resting place for the night. Not all of the night, however, as Vera gravely informed me. Little Jeremy had to get up at about 6.30 to go to school some distance away. Vera said that when that happened, of course, she had to make him some breakfast and then I would be required to leave my settee and climb into Jeremy's bed in the tiny room at the end.

It was not at all what I expected, but never mind, I settled down for a quiet little chat with Vera. It had to be quiet for her little treasure was already fast asleep. I could not chat with Beaky because he had popped out for a 'few' minutes with his agent. A small flicker of doubt as to the wisdom of staying here at all came and went. The hours passed slowly by.

Vera and I ran out of things to talk about. What she knew about theatricals was very little indeed and what I knew about golf and child rearing could be written entirely on a broken fingernail with a thick nibbed pen. But we kept up a civilized attempt at being absolutely fascinated with one another. Civilized behaviour ceased at 11.30 precisely.

There was a lot of giggling and crashing about outside the front door. After several attempts a key was successfully inserted and Beaky reeled into the room. Not far behind him, shiny with excess, was his agent Clive, a man of uncertain years, and even more uncertain gait gripping a broken daffodil between expensive teeth. Beaky and I embraced in true luvvies fashion. He apologized profusely and somewhat repetitively for being late, but told me he had been on a tour of all his agent's properties in south west London. Had Beaky mistaken an estate agent for a theatrical agent? Apparently not, for this prodigious genius combined both professions but with what degree of success, it was difficult to divine.

Both Beaky and Clive then slumped into chairs and embarked at the same time on their night's hilarious adventures. The pubs they had visited, the wine bars, Clive's houses, how Beaky had stepped in some dog shit and had left unsavoury souvenirs of his visits all over many carpets, and how, finally they had raided a small private park for some daffodils with which to surprise Vera. Vera was duly surprised.

I could not go to bed until this amazing duo had finished their talk and the two or three bottles of red wine they had brought back with them. I attempted to hasten the process by gulping down a couple or more glasses quite quickly which was an extremely unwise course of action on an empty stomach and after a long journey. In any case, it did not shorten the evening one little bit. At last around two thirty, however, Clive, his left eye gently closing, weaved his way homeward. Beaky and Vera retired to their room. I lay down thankfully on my settee, but sleep just would not come. Cigarette smoke hanging like a fog in the tiny room was stinging my eyes and irritating my throat, the smell of alcohol was everywhere. The wine I had drunk lay heavy on my stomach and what about my speech for the morning?

Many options about this began to spin round in my befuddled brain. Yes, I absolutely had to avoid the usual list of thank yous, that was certain. Instead I would recount an irreverent and funny anecdote to make them all giggle. Yes. I would tell them a rather risqué one about the famous film director going in his Rolls-Royce to get his senior cameraman from the mobile toilet. When he called out to him to get his arse on to the set the cameraman replied ... I had just decided on this, and was rehearsing mentally the form of words I would use, when the door of the front bedroom burst open and Beaky, totally naked, thundered past en route for the bathroom, knocking the kettle off the cooker and several books off the bookshelf as he went. Hard on his heels came the delectable Vera, something diaphanous streaming out behind her. 'Oh God,' she muttered, rather indistinctly for her, 'he's going to be ill.' Indeed he was, and that at length, with much groaning and moaning and further invocations of the deity.

Jeremy woke and got up to see what the fuss was about.

Vera tried to pacify him gently at the same time as remonstrating loudly with Beaky who was hugging the porcelain all this while. It was an unedifying and noisy interlude and it took a long time for things to settle down but, at last, settle down they did. I looked at my watch, it was 4.14 am. The next thing I knew, Vera was shaking me roughly by the shoulder and telling me to get up and go to Jeremy's room and thither I dutifully went. The bed was tiny I remember and there was a Mister Men duvet and a Mister Men pillowcase. There were also many pieces of Lego cunningly concealed in the bed and a teddy bear under the pillow. An indefinable smell hung about the room, but I was too tired to care very much. I curled up foetus like and closed my eyes, reckoning on a good two hours slumber. It was not to be. The wall between the child's bedroom and the bathroom against which the bed was placed was extremely thin. Jeremy was sitting on the loo and, in the fashion of lavatory training prescribed by all the advanced magazines, desperately wanted his mother to be with him at this important time in his life. Unfortunately Vera was engaged in preparing his breakfast so could not come immediately. Indeed she could not come for a long time. Little Jeremy, not used to this degree of inattention at such moving moments, began to shout, extremely loudly for one so small. When this did not work he started to howl like a wolf at a full moon and when this did not work he began to cry histrionically. Vera, harassed and upset, having had very little sleep herself, finally arrived. A furious row ensued between mother and son.

Sleep was impossible this time, so I put my hands over my ears and tried mentally to rehearse my speech. They left at 7.20 am. The silence was almost tangible. I closed my eyes. There was a banging on the door. It was Beaky, wrapped in

I curled up fœtus like ...

an ancient dressing-gown, fag in the corner of the mouth, miraculously recovered from the night's traumas, bringing me a cup of lemon tea and telling me it was probably time to get up. I burnt my lip on the tea. I stumbled through the toy aeroplanes and the Lego castles to the bathroom. The mirror told an awful tale. I might just as well have been in the Shaftesbury all night with a gang of ne'er-do-wells: the eyes were bloodshot, the complexion blotchy, the hair was standing on end and the shoulders were sagging. I was unfit for the Hilton. Meanwhile in the kitchen, Beaky had generously tried his hand at making some toast. He had burnt it but we scraped at it manfully and sat down in the remains of last night's fug to breakfast.

It was then he produced his photograph albums, a complete pictorial record of a British Council tour of one of the gloomier Shakespeare plays in which Beaky had played a minor part. I needed quiet to rehearse my potentially very funny speech. I needed to get to the Hilton but I could not be rude to dear old Beaky. He kindly showed me page after page after page of blurred photographs featuring himself and other members of the cast I had never heard of, lounging about in totally and utterly anonymous places. Every picture told a story, or rather Beaky told a story, and at length. At the point Beaky informed me that he also had a video of the last night party in Kuala Lumpur, I finally found the courage to say that I really had to go and that I had enjoyed myself greatly and I thanked him for his hospitality and I hoped it would not be another two years before we saw each other again and maybe one day, who knew, we might work together on a block-buster movie. With that I fled to a taxi rank and to the hotel. I put the finishing touches to my speech in the back of the cab. It would be a very funny, unusual and memorable speech with none of that drooling, sentimental servility so often evinced by MCs on such occasions.

My agent, beautiful and exotically dressed was waiting for me in the foyer. 'You're a bit late, but never mind,' said she, taking my arm and guiding me through the great swing doors. 'You look very smart,' she added diplomatically. This gave me a degree of confidence. I glanced round the crowded room and everywhere I looked I saw really famous people. Phil Collins, Beryl Reid, Anthony Hopkins, Peggy Ashcroft, and there in the corner – could it be, yes it was – the great Jimmy Tarbuck. Oh bliss – I had arrived.

Lunch was served. I permitted myself a glass of wine. The presentation of awards was upon us. Terry Wogan, sartorially exquisite, amazingly tanned and professionally poised, made the introductions. Celebrities began to mount the stage one by one to receive their awards. Peggy Ashcroft was suddenly before us. She made an impassioned and articulate appeal for beleaguered English theatres. Another great actor told a simple and moving story about the nature of fame and integrity. Saint and Greevsie indulged in some very funny dialogue. As the moment approached for me to arise from my chair, my confidence began to evaporate. How would my performance rank with what had gone before? How could I compete? I could not hear what my agent was saying to me but I could feel the perspiration on my forehead. I remembered the toad and the front door vividly – so great the expectation, so awful the reality, so marvellous the theory, so tragic the practise. Was my speech that funny?

'And the BBC Personality of the Year is John Nettles'. My agent was clapping me and kissing me on the cheek. I rose unsteadily. It must be the heat. All that sun. The TV camera was following me closely as I forced my way between the tables to the stage. What had the cameraman said to the director? Why had the toad been so stupid? What was the director's name? I found myself on the stage. My prepared speech disappeared from sight much as Leonie had disappeared that awful night so long ago. 'Ladies and gentlemen,' I began, gripping my silver award as if it were a lifeline, 'I would like to thank the people of Jersey, all of them, for putting up with me. I would also like to thank my fellow actors, the directors, cameramen, writers, make up artists and wardrobe. In particular I would like to thank Robert Banks Stewart for giving me the chance to . . .' etc. etc. etc.

'Good speech,' said my agent loyally, as I regained my seat.

8
Homeland

'... the isle is full of noises,
Sounds and sweet airs, that give delight, and hurt not!'
The Tempest

Well, not always. Come the high and glorious summer, the southern Jersey air is full of the snarl of traffic, the howls of ghetto-blasters and the shrieks from the crowded beaches. And come the night, the unlovely sounds of rap and drunkenness from the seething fleshpots of St Helier, so expressive of the young Brits abroad – all totty, tantrums and lager. And then there are the nightclubs with 'live' performers, though sometimes it is difficult to be sure.

It has to be said that some of the entertainment in the island is a bit down-market, the venues being less than salubrious; and some of the performers, well past their sell-by date; and some of the actors who appear here may indeed hold as 'twere the mirror up to nature, but seem in desperate need of a few pints of Windowlene. I remember taking my agent to a dimly lit nightspot in St Helier which epitomized this unfortunate aspect of Jersey life. When we stepped on to the ageing carpet it squelched. Residual quantities of lager were blamed. There was a strong smell of industrial disinfectant, gamely fighting a losing battle against a lethal cocktail of alcohol, urine, cigarette smoke and cheap perfume. The comic came from the very fundament of the provincial circuit and embarked on a series of secondhand racist and sexist jokes of extreme antiquity and so obscene as to make that comic cassowary Bernard Manning appear positively benign. We were helped in our appreciation of this bundle of comedic skills by blasts of taped laughter from speakers situated some distance behind the sparse audience. This was unnerving and debilitating enough, and my agent, whom I so wanted to impress, looked glum, but worse was to follow.

The weird gentleman in a yellow suit and Afro hairdo suddenly arched his back, and raised his arms above his head, his hands bent backwards. For a split second he held this position, eyes closed, rigid in the bright-pink spot, then, swifter than a lion falling on its prey, his arms came down in a half-circle, his fingers made contact with the keyboard and the shiny black plastic Yamaha organ roared into life. The drummer, a somewhat older man with less hair, joined in with furious rolls on the timpani. We clung fast to our lager under this onslaught. Our bijou table-lamp vibrated strangely and a curiously disembodied voice rose above the din to tell us in ecstatic tones that a singer no one had ever heard of was about to transport us into a magic world of romance, love and desire. Thunderous clapping from the speakers behind us greeted this announcement. The noise level became intense, the tension unbearable. Suddenly, from the left, a figure hurtled on stage. Just time to notice his suave three-piece suit with the chunky fob chain, the immovable battleship-grey hair swept dramatically back from the temples, the deep-mahogany tan and the ample use of eyeliner, before he launched into 'Born Free, Free as the

100

Nitelife

Wind Blows'. He then very dramatically flicked his head to the right and upwards, the better to deliver the line 'Free as the Grass Grows ...' It was at this point that he and his teeth parted company, they flying off into the dim recesses of stage right. With judicious and commendable improvisatory skill, he hummed the next two or three lines while grovelling about in the dark to retrieve and replace his precious property. Mission accomplished, he smiled a defiantly glinting smile and performed the second half of the song with more than usual emotion. I thought he was very brave and clapped along with the taped applause and tried to drown the more ribald attempts at humour from some boisterous members of the crowd. But the damage had been done. The evening had been ruined. References to strange sexual practices were insupportable and my agent, looking distinctly glum and disapproving, said she had to leave. She even used the F word, which is very unusual for her. There was nothing to say, nothing to do, but pack our tents and go, which we did.

But with a little imagination and a good map, the more sophisticated visitor can get away from all of this to the gentler reaches of this incredibly beautiful island where it is so still and quiet you could believe there was hardly a soul around for a hundred miles. And in such a place I live, in an old granite farmhouse overlooking one of those narrow, verdant valleys that run from the north of the island down to the blue waters of St Aubin Bay. It is idyllic. From my windows as I write this I can see the horses moving slowly up the dappled path towards me, little clouds of dust around their feet; two or three rabbits still as stones in the short grass of the paddock; and summer birds everywhere. And from the yard I can hear the sound of the cockerel, trying yet again for another unlikely act of congress with our compliant black duck. It seems unlikely, almost as unlikely as being able to live here with very few of the hassles and annoyances, little and large, that can dog the life of an MC elsewhere.

The reason for this pleasant state of affairs is not far to seek. Jersey is a small island, with a not very large population. Everyone knows everyone else. I am as well known in the community as Jack from the grocer's, or Nick the taxi driver, or Gabrielle the miraculously thighed, gloriously athletic movement teacher. Come to think of it, Gabrielle is probably marginally more famous than I am on this island, which is as it should be in a world somewhat short of beauty. I could be very famous across the known world (a vicar introducing me at a fête did indeed remark, 'in some places he is known worldwide') but it would matter little in Jersey, for that world is merely a suburb of the island and treated with scant respect. Besides, the islands are quite used to having MCs and even properly famous people in their midst.

The list is endless. That great benefactor of the British working classes – and, incidentally, of the British actor – Sir Billy Butlin, lived here. Tony Jacklin lived here. Gilbert O'Sullivan lives here. His delightfully delicate lyricism, as expressed in such songs as 'What's in a Kiss?' and that belated but none the less welcome blow for male chauvinism 'A Woman's Place is in the Home', will surely live for ever. Talking of delicacy, the internationally renowned actor, wit, raconteur and scourge of late-night poseurs, Oliver Reed, lives just across the way on our sister island of Guernsey. And those two legends of the leather and willow world, John Arlott and Ian Botham, live at least some of the time out on Alderney. Derek Warwick, the racing driver, lives in the next parish to me and, of course, the celebrated Alan Whicker resides over on the east of the island.

Alan Whicker is as entertaining and amusing off-screen as he is on, and lives in the most delightful house, hidden in trees above a quiet bay. On the first occasion I went to dine with the great man, I remember (just) staggering off to the loo full of an excellent if heady claret and a quantity of even more excellent salmon and Jersey Royals. I observed blearily that he had hung many lists of best-selling books around the small room. It didn't matter if you were sitting or standing, you could always see those lists of best-sellers, in which A.W.'s books figured to great effect.

This is not a strange practice, or at least it is no stranger than the practice of an actor friend of mine who has arranged a series of photographs of himself in various dramatic roles all turned towards the loo, which is raised on a kind of podium. It is a most disconcerting and unnerving experience to face this grinning collection when one is at one's most vulnerable, and I find the whole arrangement distressing and unsuitable. I flatter myself that I am much kinder to my guests, many of whom share my profession. There is said to be an ancient Chinese adage which goes as follows: 'Happiness is to have much money, many friends, an adoring wife, lovely children and occasionally to see your neighbour fall off the roof.' This is probably neither ancient nor Chinese, but it does contain more than a kernel of truth, so, bearing this in mind, I have adorned the walls of my loo with some of my more spectacularly bad reviews – a bad review being the thespian equivalent of unwished-for and precipitate tumbling from the tiles. In the privacy of the loo, my honoured guests may read them at their leisure, have a good giggle, feel immediately superior and emerge, therefore, a much more social animal. Nothing awakens good humour more than other people's misfortunes.

Another Jersey resident, one Harry Patterson, has a great fortune – many millions of pounds, it is whispered. His considerable wealth has been amassed from the sales of his hugely popular books, written under the name of Jack Higgins. Such titles as *The Eagle Has Landed*, *The Eagle Has Flown*, *Prayer for the Dying*, *Cold Harbour* and *Night of the Fox* have shot into the best-seller lists with almost indecent ease and can be found all round the world. Unlike many rich immigrants who cloister themselves away behind thick walls and make no contribution to the social life of Jersey, Harry is a very accessible person. His wit, mercifully not confined to his novels, and his colourful narrative style, guaranteed to enthral listeners, make him much sought after in the literary and brighter social circles of the island.

He also sings very well. I discovered this by accident when, in search of spiritual entertainment, I invited him, a jolly policeman I know who must remain anonymous for career reasons (my career, that is, not his; the noble officer has rather a lot on me and I don't want to be catching the mailboat just yet) and my friend Philip Forster along to a night of rock and roll nostalgia with Simon Raverne and his band at the Malton Hotel. I don't know why I invited Phil, since he is a devilish handsome sort of chap and tends to put me a little in the shade with his sophisticated humour and *savoir faire*. But there we were, I and my girlfriend, they and their wives, at the Malton, and I knew we were in for a good night. Simon Raverne, strikingly grey, tall, mature and confident, a rocker of some distinction from the 1960s and a novelist in his own right, met us in the foyer, asking us politely not to sign autographs while he was in the middle of his act. We solemnly agreed not to do so and our merry little band trooped into the cabaret room.

This night was going to be special, different; not an air-borne denture in sight. Yes, it was going to be good. A small flicker of doubt surfaced when we saw the rest of the audience, who inexplicably all stood up as we entered. Now, at least as far as outward appearances were concerned, we were reasonably mature adults in our mid-forties or there-abouts, but the rest of the company for the night was posi-tively ancient – lovely, but ancient. As we took our places, armed with lagers and a quantity of crisps, on the tastefully designed PVC-covered seats, we gazed across a veritable sea of white hair to the small stage. Would these ranks of venerable seniority respond to the youthful charm and, more importantly, to the rock and roll music of Simon Raverne, that astonishing reincarnation of the 1960s? A hush descended, but whether that was the hush of expectancy or the hush that comes to older people after a long, sun-filled day riding around in hot coaches and walking on the sand, I could not tell. At that moment, though, all rumination was cut short as the house lights dimmed and old snake-hips Raverne himself appeared, fittingly attired in a garb of luminous white material.

As the first rock number, driving twelve-bar blues with the accent very much on the off-beat, hit the air, I surreptitiously glanced about me. The serried rows of senior citizens were not exactly being swept off their feet. Some of them, it is true to say, were nodding, but again, impossible to tell if they were nodding to the beat or just nodding off – though the latter was unlikely, given the noise. Others sat quite still, crunching the occasional crisp and gazing morosely at their small drinks. I realized, through a mounting alcoholic haze, that these good people were not rock and roll addicts who had come from miles around to see their hero; they just happened to be guests at the hotel who couldn't think of anything else to do. In an ideal world they would have preferred to be at an Ann Shelton concert, or a Billy Cotton Band Show, or indeed anywhere else in the world apart from the Malton Hotel with an MC, a best-selling novelist and a rock and roll singer, no matter how good he was. And Simon was good. He soldiered on with considerable aplomb, and much flailing of the arms and shaking of the legs, after the fashion of the Memphis King himself. Here was the hair, dropping in wild abandon over provocative, half-closed eyes, the sensuous lips twisted round such knottily difficult locutions as 'Let me be your teddy bear, uh huh huh, uh huh huh, yea yea' and 'Comealonga mumma a whole lotta shakin' goin' on'.

A zimmer moved gently behind me. A mottled hand came to rest on my shoulder and above the noise, a charming octogenarian shouted with surprising force directly into my ear: 'Would you sign this for me, please?' He thrust a paper napkin into my hand. I took the napkin and began signing but

107

suddenly remembered Simon's pre-show strictures about giving autographs while he was performing. I glanced up guiltily to see if the vintage rocker was observing me, and if he was, whether he would be inclined to arrange his guitar round my neck. I need not have worried. Simon, a moving testimony to the belief that there is life after forty, was just reaching a climax in a really fab number. His head was thrown back, a patina of perspiration was making the well-formed features glow in the spotlight, the knees were pointing together and the guitar was held more in hope than anger at a provocative 45-degree angle from the groin. I don't think he was observing anything very much at all. I hastily completed my signature (reflecting yet again on the silliness of being called Nettles) and handed it back to the wizened fan. Only he wasn't a fan after all.

'It's not for me,' he roared. 'I hate the bloody show. It's for the Missus. She likes you for some reason I don't understand.'

With that he shuffled off. Unworthy thoughts of euthanasia flashed across my fevered brain. Mercifully I could not entertain them for long, since Harry, surfing on great waves of nostalgia, grabbed me by the knee as the wonderfully supple Simon was shake, rattle and rolling to one of the more famous Elvis Presley numbers. We joined in, our faces closer than is allowed the heterosexual British male in any other circumstance, Harry taking the melody line and myself essaying the harmony in thirds. My singing is as good as my dancing, which is to say it's terrible, but Harry's was very good indeed, and it was curious that, with his dark glasses and black hair combed forward, he had more than a little of Roy Orbison about him.

It was at this point of high euphoria that I emptied half a pint of lager into my lap. Not that it mattered very much,

Harry and I were having a whale of a time, reliving our youth – 'no more behind but such a day tomorrow as today, and to be boy eternal'. Even Philip, usually gravely and responsibly calm and terribly reserved in an English sort of way, loosened his cravat and tapped an elegantly brogued toe more or less in time with the music. As for our policeman chum, he too was singing along, strangely well informed as to the lyrics of late 1950s and early 1960s pop songs. On such rafts of trivia were we all launched towards adulthood. Small wonder some of us failed miserably to make the journey.

After an hour our voices were hoarse with all the coloratura singing and our faces red and glistening with the liberal intake of beer. We were ecstatically happy. Simon finally ended the show and my party swayed to its feet to applaud vociferously such an invocation of our nursery experience. The rest of the audience, who unlike us had observed the entire show in respectful silence, would, I am sure, have done the same had they been able to. As it was, they either clapped politely or just gazed at our hero in what I took to be open-mouthed adoration. The show over, I was besieged by our elderly friends asking to have their photographs taken with me. My lady friend, who seemed strangely annoyed with life at this point, whispered ferociously in my ear that my earlier mishap with the lager had left a large, damp stain on my trousers and that this would be open to mis-interpretation when it appeared on dozens of photographs. While objecting somewhat to her tone, I none the less recognized the truth of her observation and hastily sat down behind a table to have my photo taken.

It had been a good night. I weaved my way finally towards my homebound taxi, on my own as the girlfriend had already left. I think she was a little tired, what with the excitement and everything, and when, still in a state of euphoria, I arrived home she had gone to bed. In search of even more excitement I played some Dusty Springfield very loudly and finally, because I began to feel a little emotional around 2 o'clock, I played some of the more meaningful country and western tracks in my collection, ending with my all time favourite, Bobby Bare singing 'Drop-kick me, Jesus, Through the Goalposts of Life'. As it happened, that had to be the very last number for the night as the girlfriend suddenly appeared, inquiring as to my sanity and wondering whether or not anyone in the house was going to get any sleep. I decided that I preferred my own company and passed out peacefully on the sofa.

Now, all this is not to say that the life of an MC here in Jersey is a never-ending merry-go-round of juvenile self-indulgence. I don't want you to get the impression that I spend my entire life chomping my way through unlimited quantities of lotus. Far from it. Along with the pleasures and the privileges go the duties and obligations – though these too can be pleasurable, such as presenting gala shows with David Jacobs and Richard Baker, who are two very grown-up people, and on one memorable occasion being presented to Her Majesty the Queen and Prince Philip.

I think that this latter was in my capacity as an ambassador for island tourism, but be that as it may I was hugely and properly excited at the prospect. I spent hours practising attitudes and bows, merry quips and different voices with which to impress Her Majesty. In moments of vaulting and impossible ambition I even dreamed of being dubbed Sir John of St Ouen. So it was with great anticipation that I and the rest of our little island community waited for the great day of the Queen's visit to dawn. Practical problems first?

What to wear? Since I had been clothed almost exclusively by the BBC wardrobe department for the previous seven years, I had very few modish clothes of my own. Moreover, those I did have did not fit all that well, as I had recently been putting on some weight, particularly round the neck and shoulders. I tried both my suits but they were too small, particularly, I have to say, the trousers; my waist had expanded too. At length I hit upon the answer. I would wear the dark-blue blazer, which was only a little too small, and the grey slacks with shiny brown shoes. This sartorial display would indicate beyond a shadow of doubt that the wearer was a responsible, mature adult, properly respectful of the British establishment. Further inspiration – I would wear my RNLI tie, kindly presented to me by the lads down at the harbour, and this would be proof positive, if any more were needed, of my outstanding integrity and commitment to decent, civilized behaviour. The final touch would be my nice cuff-links, which are blue, with a compass and what looks like a set square motif inset in gold. The shirt would, of course, be white, but none I had fitted easily. I decided to buy the shirt on the very day of the Queen's visit so it would be fresh from the cellophane, like those of Hurricane Higgins.

My official invitation arrived. I was to be a member of a party from Jersey tourism presented to Her Majesty in a marquee in the parish of St Lawrence at around 2.30, and would I bring the Triumph Roadster, please. The Triumph Roadster? But the old girl had been much used that summer of 1989, what with car-chase sequences and the hundreds of tourists who had been sitting in her. As a result, there was a long split in the leatherwork on her front seat. This was, to say the least, unsightly, and it was certainly unfit for the sight of our reigning monarch. Immediate representations were made to George Gallaccio to provide the necessary funds to effect a suitable repair.

Now George, as the producer of *Bergerac*, works for the cash-strapped BBC. It is easier to get water from a desert-baked stone, easier to get a kind remark about Margaret from Edward Heath, than it is to extract money from George. 'But she won't look inside the car,' he remarked dismissively, rather undervaluing the whole occasion, I thought. 'So there is no point in doing much more than cover the tear with some gaffer tape.' His other suggestion of throwing a rug or blanket over the front seat I thought equally unhelpful and also, in some vague way, treasonable. Fortunately, that great polymath and fixer, Kevin from Jersey, cut the Gordian knot, got the repair done properly and added the cost to that of the old car's very necessary annual service. So that was all right. I was sure I would be fully and properly prepared for the great event, but – again – I was mistaken in my assumption.

The day of the Queen's visit dawned and it was the most perfect sunlit day imaginable. I rose early to take Alice, our dog, down to a sea already dazzlingly blue beneath a cloudless sky. I returned to my old farmhouse for a bite to eat and then set off for the shops to buy the white shirt and also some black socks. This was when I realized I had made my first major mistake. All the shops were closed for the Queen's visit. There wasn't the remotest possibility of purchasing a white shirt, let alone black socks, anywhere on the island. I thought of borrowing one from my friend Sean Arnold (who plays Inspector Crozier in the series), but a moment's reflection made me see what an absurd notion this was. Sean is an amiable fellow, possessed of great wit and charm, but he can fairly be said to be sartorially anarchic. There was as much likelihood of Sean having a decent white shirt as a rabbi having a leg of pork in the deep freeze. I had to find another solution, and quickly.

I tried on several of my old shirts and found one, thank God, that almost fitted. I could just about fasten the top button, though this pinched my neck abominably and caused some constriction to my vocal cords, leaving speech more than a little difficult. I didn't imagine Her Majesty would particularly enjoy the company of a half-strangled thespian who could hardly articulate. Then I remembered a trick used by one of my dressers, Leo, who, when he wasn't slapping legs, was a mine of useful information and very inventive indeed. Faced with this same problem, Leo had simply sewn the button on a long thread so that it hung a little away from the collar and could thus be fastened quite easily. I did my best to imitate this process and achieved a passable result. It still wasn't comfortable, but it was comfortable enough, although it looked just a little odd. I planned to disguise everything by tying my RNLI tie in a more than usually large knot. This proved a little difficult, because I was understandably nervous and a little sweaty. I kept tying the tie wrongly, in that the back strip of tie, which is not meant to be seen, poked out somewhere below the front strip, which is meant to be seen. Finally I got it right. I then cut off the bottoms of a pair of my daughter's black tights to provide the requisite black socks and embarked on the last operation – fixing the cuff-links. Now, man has been many thousands of years upon this planet and breathtaking technical and scientific advantages have been made – we can dance upon the moon and gaze wonderingly into the deepest corners of the universe – yet we still have cuff-links. Half an hour later, fingertips bruised and nails split, I finally got my curiously designed cuff-links correctly positioned. Last-minute shock – I had no shoe polish. Still, I lightly rubbed some cooking oil over my footwear, which proved to be very successful.

Off I went in haste to St Lawrence, which was very crowded and very hot. I took my place in the marquee with a score or so of sweating dignitaries, men in grey suits, women in impossibly formal dresses, all waiting to be presented. The Royal party was late, so I had time to take a look about. A number of plain-clothes policemen I recognized from the Jersey force were lurking about, as well as a number of rather large fellows in well-cut grey suits with curious bulges under their left armpits. They were on the move all the time, continually watching, poised. There was a large crowd of *hoi polloi* outside the marquee, all jostling to get near the front. I noticed one local politician who was obviously taking the Queen's visit very seriously indeed, to the extent that he had changed his whole appearance. His greying hair, previously combed forward, was now swept magnificently away from his forehead and straight back over the top of the head, coming to rest just above the back of his collar. A black streak ran fetchingly down the centre. He looked curiously like a frightened badger. Next to me and the beautifully repaired Triumph was the clever chef from L'Horizon hotel (a somewhat different class of establishment to the aforementioned Malton), who had created a wondrous sculpture in chocolate of a cockerel and hen and their eggs; it sat magnificent on a table in front of him. Further into the marquee were representatives of agriculture, standing in front of stalls of Jersey produce, and beyond them was the prize Jersey cow herd.

It was exceedingly hot. The button on my shirt fell off. As I tightened my tie to hold the collar together, the back strip of the tie appeared again. This time I tucked it inside my shirt. I could smell the cows, even from this distance. The chef was gazing rather anxiously at his fabulous creation, which was getting very shiny and losing a little definition in the roasting heat. A senator, whose name I have diplomatically forgotten, strolled over to me and said: 'John, when you are presented, do you think you could manoeuvre Her Majesty a little into the sunshine, so that we can get a better picture for tourism.' I thought about this, but not for long. As a career move, it appeared to be a mistake, for though I am not an expert, I believe that manhandling the Sovereign can be a head-losing exercise. I made a mental note not to do any such thing. I also remembered that I would only bow to Her Majesty and Prince Philip and to no one else. I had been presented to Princess Alexandra a couple of years previously and had bowed to everyone, but everyone, in the party. I was busy bowing before Gyles Brandreth

115

when that great man kindly pointed out to me that I was being a bit silly. A salutary experience that – wouldn't do it again.

But suddenly there was no more time for thought. There was the Royal party, just beyond the entrance of the tent. A hush fell over the crowd. It was as if everyone was holding their breath. From where I stood, sweat dripping down the inside of my shirt, I could see the Queen and the Prince being introduced to the herd of cows. Behind the Royals stood the Bailiff, Sir Peter Crill – very formal, very upright, attired in what must have been very hot, black, medieval dress. The party progressed slowly through the marquee, very slowly. The badger man shifted uneasily from foot to foot. The formally dressed ladies were now glowing furiously. The chef kept eyeing the melting chocolate and I could feel my collar separating from my neck.

Then it was my turn to be presented. The Queen turned from admiring the beauteous melting charms of the chocolate sculpture and advanced towards me. Her Majesty did look closely into the car. Her Majesty spoke kindly to me. I would willingly have died for her.

'And you have got your housing qualifications to live in Jersey?'

'Oh yes,' said I.

'And about time too,' said Her Majesty.

Sir Peter Crill, saintlike behind her, smiled. Or was it a grimace? Impossible to tell.

Prince Philip bustled up, opining that he was surprised anybody came to Jersey at all, given the appalling rate of crime as it appeared in *Bergerac*. We all laughed – my, how we laughed! The president of tourism came out with the pithy observation that the storylines were fiction but the scenery was real. Everyone looked impressed and nodded

The cooking oil had soaked into the leather of my shoes.

sagely at this, and then it was all over. The Royal party moved on. I was left on my own. I looked down and saw that the cooking oil had soaked into the leather of my shoes, turning them a mottled black. A few minutes later I realized that I still had a smile on my face, and who could blame me? I drove home in a dream, changed from my sodden clothes, had a large, very large, glass of white wine, cycled down to the beach and swam for the whole of the afternoon. Then, as the sun set slowly over Guernsey, I went for a long walk along the wide harp of the bay, my footsteps leaving large puddles in the yielding sands as I listened to Cliff Richard on my Walkman. Perhaps it had been a dream, but if so, it surely beat the hell out of real life.

9
The Charity Roundabout

'... We are born to do benefits
And what better or properer can we call our own than
the riches of our friends.'

Timon of Athens

There are more charities than there are actors in work, more worthy causes than decent plays, and more requests to appear at fund-raising events than fan letters. When our MC is not appearing on cheap game shows, or getting a lot of money for opening supermarkets (not so much cash in hand nowadays – the boys from the Inland Revenue got wise to that), he or she can be found at the 'charity event'. In my experience, this can take a thousand forms, mostly, but not always, pleasant. Here in Jersey, I and the rest of the celebrities spend many a happy afternoon at fêtes, of which there are a great number, during the long hot summers.

Holidaymakers – mostly from mainland Britain, as we call it, but with more than a smattering from Scandinavia, Holland and Australia – always, without exception, prove very generous indeed and will donate anything up to ten pounds each in return for a picture of the famous if antique Triumph Roadster. The money raised goes to Jersey Hospice Care, which is a good thing. Everyone has a laugh, which is also a good thing. I can play to larger audiences than many performers will ever see, and that, I must confess, is the best thing of all. It is all highly satisfactory.

However, not all charity events are as pleasant. Indeed, one sort of charity event can often be positively damaging to the health. I speak of the charity show which takes place in a real theatre in front of a paying audience, often composed, unnervingly enough, of friends and loved ones. I hate having friends and loved ones watch me on the stage in such shows, if only because of the pain they go through trying to find the precise superlatives to describe my performance, when I and they know that it was truly and awesomely awful.

My friend David Schofield, who is a seriously good actor (but I am not jealous), has discovered a way through the awful problem that occurs when confronting a perspiring thespian chum after you have just spent three hours of agony watching a performance of such appalling ineptitude as to beggar description. Instead of coming straight out and saying, 'I would rather have live ferrets thrust down my trousers than sit through that mountain of ordure', one crouches a little, opens wide the mouth in the semblance of a smile, points a finger at the end of an extended arm straight at the expectant thespian and then, after a second's dramatic pause, cries, 'You old bastard, you've done it again!' Now, the beauty is that this can mean what you want it to. The speaker doesn't have to spoil a perfectly good friendship by telling a hurtful truth. The roseate actor, on the other hand, face full of removing cream, can hear that he was absolutely super and divine, that his cover hasn't yet been blown.

I pass this information on to you, dear reader, in a charitable way so that you may benefit should you find yourself in such a situation and wish to compromise neither your own integrity nor your friendship with the performer. I myself used to say just, 'Thank you', which is possessed of the same ambiguity but lacks a little of the colour of David's line, which I have now adapted as my own invention.

'You old bastard, you've done it again!'

One has to be armed thus on all theatrical occasions in the melancholy event of the performance falling somewhat short of expectation. Charity shows usually do fall short in this way, and the reasons why are not far to seek. For any number of different reasons, the artists cannot all be brought together to rehearse properly either their own act itself or the way it fits into the running order. Consequently, everything is done not even at the last minute but the last second before curtain-up. There are always too many acts, because the organizers have asked too many people to take part and they've all said yes. And if there is anything to go wrong, it will go wrong. For all the above reasons, charity shows go on far, far too long. This was certainly true of the one into which I was

121

inveigled at the Tivoli Gardens in Copenhagen some years ago.

1970 was the year in which I first became an MC, obviously not for playing Bergerac but for playing a morose and, as it turned out, impotent gynaecologist, one Dr Ian Mackenzie, in the lenten soap opera *Family at War*, which on occasion got better ratings than *Coronation Street*. (What *Eastenders* was to the late 1980s, *Family at War* was to the early 1970s.) The series was also a big hit in Denmark, to the point where one of its stars, Colin Campbell, almost became an honorary citizen. It was he who first had the idea of putting on the charity show, and a producer/director whom we will call Dickie Hump to protect his reputation was employed to put the whole thing together. Now, this had to be a mistake, for, although in normal circumstances a very good man to have on your side, as far as organizing this show was concerned, he had as much chance as getting a sun-tan in a pot-hole. Not that we were much better. Myself and fellow luminaries from the soap (including that lovely actress Barbara Flynn, later famous for many fine performances, including that in the *Biederbecke Affair*) gathered to rehearse what we considered to be exquisitely clever sketches, ending with a walk-down routine in which we sang a medley of wartime songs.

A plane was chartered, and off we flew to the bitterly cold Danish capital. On the plane I looked at the rest of the performers. At first I thought there was nothing untoward. Sitting within touching distance were the legendary Hatti Jacques and John Le Mesurier, not to mention Joe Brown and his new group, Home Brew – intimations of quality indeed. But then doubts began to creep in. The rest of the party was made up of hirsute and raucous pop singers, one-hit wonders to a man, and there were a lot of them.

Apparently no one had turned down the invitation to appear and so we had enough acts to do ten shows, let alone one.

The flight was a troubled affair. A quantity of tinned beer was consumed, not to mention other less legal substances. The assembled musicians decided to have a singsong and the pilot had gently to dissuade them from stamping rigorously and rhythmically on the floor of the aircraft; as he explained in a curiously tight voice, such pounding threatened the safety of the aircraft and therefore wasn't a particularly good idea. The assembled popsters eventually complied with much cavilling and not a little incivility.

The plane arrived late and we hurried off, some making for the fleshpots of Copenhagen, others – more tired and possibly more timorous – making for the comfort of the hotel and a good night's sleep. Our little *Family at War* act was due to rehearse at 2 o'clock the following afternoon. Come the morning, myself and one of the actresses were interviewed by a journalist. I use the term loosely – he was a smiling, mendacious peddler of sensation and untruth of the kind we, of course, don't have in this country, the sort of journalist who would write headlines like SEX-STARVED STAR YEARNS FOR ELUSIVE LOVER if you happened to mention that you were single and might consider getting married if the right woman came along some time. It passed and we walked around the cold capital just to get some fresh air, and finally arrived at the theatre at 2 o'clock sharp.

The Tivoli Garden Theatre was a massively impressive affair, with a very large stage quite big enough to put on full-scale opera or ballet. The seating capacity was huge, running into thousands, I seem to remember, and very luxurious. However, rehearsals for the evening's charity gala were not going too well. Banks of loudspeakers were being set up along the front of the stage and the engineers seemed to be

123

having a great deal of trouble getting the sound level right. Dickie Hump, dressed in a multi-coloured sweater and looking disconcertingly like Ken Russell berating a film critic, was speeding up and down the aisles, gesticulating wildly and shouting about something, though precisely what we couldn't tell. Slumped in a corner of the auditorium we saw the *Guardian* critic, sent along to review the performance; her name was Linda Christmas. She was very pretty but did not look very pleased.

The afternoon wore on. Time was getting short and still we were not called to rehearse our act, which was to be the grand climax of the show. The rockers were still getting the levels right. Eartha Kitt, startlingly attractive, maintained a quiet dignity in the face of yet another delay to her rehearsal time. We played cards and tried to rehearse in our dressing room, which is rather like practising for a cross-Channel swim in a bath tub. We gave that up and together with a mate, for want of anything better to do, I went for a stroll around the backstage area, to see the other dressing rooms and rehearsal areas. In one of the latter we discovered a Danish modern jazz quartet, running through their stuff. With admirable foresight we decided to ask them if they would accompany us in our walk-down selection of wartime songs at the end of our act. At first there was, unusually, some little difficulty explaining exactly what we wanted. So we summoned Isabella, the girl who had been assigned to help us sort out any problems. She explained perfectly our needs, and even hummed a line or two of 'I Like a Nice Cup of Tea in the Morning' to assist the veteran minstrels in their endeavours to assist us. They very kindly agreed to help. Gathering as many members of our team as possible, we planned to have a little rehearse; this was cut short after about five minutes because our newfound friends had to go down to the stage. We thought our piece would be all right.

The show was billed to start at 7.30 and it was getting awfully late. 6.30 rolled by and still we hadn't had our rehearsal. At last we were called, but had little time to do anything more than run quickly through what we were intending to do. We also ran through the songs we were to sing at the end, without our minstrels, who had retreated into their dressing rooms for cigarettes and schnapps.

Thousands of people were converging on the Tivoli. The theatre was filling up. From a vantage point high in the vaulted ceiling above the auditorium, I could discern that they were mostly sophisticated middle-aged and elderly people, all quite conservatively dressed, who probably remembered the wartime years very well indeed. There were some young people there, it is true, but not many.

Miraculously, the show started only ten minutes later than advertised. The ambassadors, diplomats, states persons and assorted dignitaries were all safely in their seats. The lights dimmed and two spots slashed through the darkness to pick out the two compères standing either side of the stage. For pity's sake I will not name them, but they embarked on patter which would have been entirely at home in the unwashed mouth of a third-form schoolboy but certainly not here. Their repartee reached a frenzy of creativity in the following exchange, spoken very slowly, the better to enable the ignorant Danes to enjoy the joke.

A: What's the difference between a snowman and a snowwoman?
B: I don't know. What is the difference between a snowman and a snowwoman?
A: Snowballs.

A nuclear winter could not have provided a more surreal

silence. One of the compères, thinking that there was a language difficulty, repeated the tagline – 'snowballs!' he cried, making shapes in the air with his hands, the better to convey the meaning of what he was saying. There was an almost imperceptible murmur from the huge audience, like a breeze through the grass. This was the sound of people who had come to see Pavarotti and found Jess Conrad, come to be entertained and found themselves insulted. If there was an excuse for this lumpen vulgarity, I don't know what it was. It was certainly a bit late in the day to exact revenge for having to pay Danegeld.

Worse followed in the shape of a six-strong pop group, all with flowing locks and beards, who barged through a set of songs which all sounded exactly like 'Tie a Yellow Ribbon Round the Old Oak Tree'. And all the time the volume was excruciatingly high, vibrating the eyes into double vision and hammering the eardrums into deafness. After a third number had assaulted the auditorium, I turned and fled as far away as possible for a fag and a gulp of vodka – and to reflect upon the wisdom of doing charity shows at all. Even at this distance from the scene of the crime I could feel the thudding, unchanging rhythm shaking the floor and unhinging the very doors of my dressing room.

After half an hour or so, animated by the voyeurism that makes people watch horrendous accidents, I crept back to the little gallery overlooking the auditorium to see what was happening. Much the same was happening. Yet another group, almost indistinguishable from the first, was playing another version of 'Tie a Yellow Ribbon Round the Old Oak Tree', even more loudly, if that were possible. The audience seemed totally immune to the charms of the music. There was a definite sensation of unease, a positive restiveness. The exit doors were being exercised quite vigorously. I seemed to see a bejewelled lady assaulting a sound engineer squatting before the banks of amps at the front of the stage, but I could have been mistaken in this. The two compères came on again.

A: What's Coco got that his wife hasn't?
B: I don't know. What's Coco got that his wife hasn't?
A: Coconuts.

I retreated for another shot of the Russian and another cigarette. An hour went by very slowly. I was depressed. I tried to have a little nap, but failed miserably in my attempt. Besides, I was beginning to feel more than a little light-headed. I went off for a walk and bumped into Isabella, who, I noticed, had rather lovely bright-blue eyes. She told me that the interval was at last coming up, and that Dickie Hump wanted to see all the second-half acts in the scene dock by the stage, to tell us of some last-minute alterations to the programme. I meandered down to the wings. A lot of people were milling about, another pop group was singing about yellow ribbons and old oak trees. Dickie Hump was having a furious argument with one of the Danish officials; I overheard, indeed everyone within forty yards overheard, their exchange.

'But they're going to lynch me. There are four thousand people out there and they're going to lynch me. You must cut, cut, cut!' howled the desperate official.

'I shall do no such thing,' responded Dickie, stoutly clutching a chunky glass full of clear liquid and a slice of lemon, waving a running order around his head and adding imperiously, 'Tell me who else in the fucking world could have organized this show? Nobody. I am the producer, OK? OK?'

There was an awful lot of finger-jabbing and asking of rhetorical questions before the altercation was ended as the

All charity shows go on too long.

beleaguered Dane, turning smartly on his heels, marched off. Dickie turned to Joe Brown, who happened to be nearest, and asked him to cut a few of his numbers so that the show might end at a reasonable time – that is to say, before the sun came up the following morning. He refused, for the excellent reason that nobody else was willing to shorten their act. Another argument developed. John Le Mesurier looked morose. There was more noise from another corner, where the resident stagehands were debating whether or not they would work on after twelve o'clock.

I hung around the stage for a taste of the second half, which got under way after a lengthy interval at around 10.20. It looked as if things were improving. Well, they did improve when Kathy Kirby, although she had spent an inordinate amount of time being a little less than kind to her docile dresser and companion, belted out a muscular version of 'Once I Had a Secret Love', and then a perfectly heart-rending rendition of 'My Yiddisher Momma'. Things got back to normal after she had finished her spot. The two compères appeared again.

A: My wife's so big, d'you know what she calls her bra?
B: No. What does she call her bra?
A: An over-shoulder-boulder-holder.

Another pop group came on. I left for the dressing room, sustained by the hope of another vodka and pursued up the long stairs by the strains of the song which might have been about knotting lengths of buttercup-coloured silk around a tree trunk – I was too far gone to notice really. I determined to wait in the dressing room until called, and it was a very long wait. Midnight loomed. Soon the stagehands would be on double time. They were being paid from the profits of the show, which would dwindle accordingly. At last, at 11.55 Isabella, who was perspiring rather fetchingly, appeared at the door to tell us that we were next on. I drained my glass and somewhat dizzily – because I was nervous, you understand – descended towards the stage, taking a moment off to observe what was happening in the auditorium from my little gallery. Things had deteriorated. The house lights had been left on for some reason and the audience was mostly in the bar towards the back of the theatre. Those who remained – the infirm and the teetotal – all had their hands over their ears. One woman, the same dangerous woman I had observed earlier assaulting a sound engineer, had her hands over her ears too but was also half out of her seat and was hurling abuse towards the stage, where yet another ragamuffin pop group was imperatively requesting a particular arboreal adornment at very high volume. We waited in the wings. It seemed an unconscionable time. The two compères were at it again.

A: My wife's just gone off on holiday.
B: Jamaica?
A: No. She left of her own accord.

There was silence. The auditorium had filled up to see us. Strange music, perhaps by Vaughan Williams filled the air. The crowd saw the lovely Coral Atkins appear on stage and roared and stamped their approval. Then Colin Campbell, less lovely but still adored, appeared, pretending to be a little drunk at the back of the auditorium. I was in fact a little drunk and made my entrance with the charming Barbara Flynn and others. We weren't quite so popular as the first two but we got a decent round of applause. Truth to tell, we should all have left it at that – appeared, waved to the

audience and then legged it home – but no, we had to spoil
it by performing our sketch, notable only for its outstanding
puerility and such a complete lack of humour that it made our
two benighted compères paradigms of comic inventiveness.

It had one virtue, however: its brevity. We rushed through
it breathlessly and then all lined up, feeling strangely small
on the vast Tivoli stage, for the walk-down with the medley
of wartime songs. The Danish musicians accompanied us as
they had promised to do. Only one thing was wrong: the
disagreement between them and us as to the order in which
the songs were to be sung. Because we were all concentrating
like mad on the difficult – that is, for actors – step-and-kick
routine with which we rather inappropriately accompanied
the songs, it wasn't until some way into the medley that
one of our number realized what was happening. It was
interesting to note just how bad and cacophonous it sounded
when the band were playing 'I Like a Nice Cup of Tea in
the Morning' and we were singing 'A Nightingale Sang in
Berkeley Square'. Somehow, in some way we managed to
get through. The good and kindly Danes – more in admiration, one must suppose, for our television performances
than for our present palpable ineptitude – cheered us mightily.

It was around half past one when we finished signing
autographs and chatting to the fans. A group of us went to
a discotheque in our hotel and thence to my bedroom for a
chat and a drink. Isabella, who by this time had changed
into a long, figure-hugging orange dress, was getting more
and more beautiful by the minute and I was certainly getting
wittier. The rest of the thespians were, I think, a little too
tired to appreciate my jokes and satirical barbs for very long,
and so one by one they slipped away, leaving just me and
that wicked enchantress Isabella. I recounted my life story

which she found extraordinarily interesting. She kept nodding in agreement with the points I was making and then we went to bed. I told her a few of the more choice anecdotes from my career in rep and then disappeared to the bathroom, just for a moment, to burnish the caps and do manly things like splashing the aftershave under the armpits. When I returned, Isabella was fast asleep and would not be wakened. I left her to her dreams and lay on my back for a while, reflecting on the day's events and on whether it was right in the name of charity to inflict on people a degree of suffering almost equal to that of the people for whom the charity had been set up in the first place. Finding no answer to the conundrum, I too fell into a deep, deep sleep.

The flight home was a glum affair. Dickie Hump, demonstrating remarkable powers of recuperation, did try over the Tannoy to get some community-singing going. He kicked off with 'We'll Meet Again', but nobody joined in. There were, however, some thoughtful comments as to the nature of Dickie's parentage and whether or not a person could survive a fall into the North Sea from 20,000 feet.

Linda Christmas wrote a less than ecstatic notice for the *Guardian*, calling the whole thing an expensive shambles and the efforts of the *Family at War* team in particular infantile, pathetic, unfunny and schoolboyish. I agreed with her, and vowed never to appear in a charity show again.

I broke this vow of course, almost fourteen years later, when I was again an MC. It was a foolish thing to do and I had much the same nerve-racking experience as before. It was the familiar story, with one important difference: Donald Sinden was on the bill. I have met many people in showbiz during my career and can vouch for the fact that there is a small, select band of actors and entertainers who are held in special esteem and regard by the rest of us, because of the special gifts they possess. Donald Sinden is one of that number. The sun comes out when he walks into a room. His humour, his love of life, especially theatrical life, is unparalleled in the entertainment world, his acting in roles as diverse as Foppington and King Lear, a wonder. He held court backstage at this particular charity show, which, like most such shows, went on for ever. Among many tales and jokes, he told me the following:

> A man was walking down a street, a perfectly ordinary street in a perfectly ordinary town. Suddenly a door burst open, a young man raced across the road to the opposite pavement, leapt high in the air and fell flat on his face. The man ran up to him to see if he was all right.
>
> 'What did you do that for?' he inquired of the young man.
>
> The young man replied, 'Oh, I've just got engaged and this is where I thought I'd left my bicycle.'

A Mini-Celebrity's Practical Guide to Survival

AGENTS

Generally speaking, these people are necessary, as it was once thought leeches were efficacious in curing almost all disorders. That is to say, one is not quite certain if they are of any use at all, but it's best to have one just in case. They are characterized by a species of hyperactivity, particularly when their client is in attendance, expressing itself in protracted shouting matches down the phone, rummaging in filing cabinets and rushing around the smarter or 'in' eateries to have lunch with their out-of-work clients or dinner after the show with those who are in work.

If you are unlucky enough to be out of work, then it is always a bad time of year. 'But my dear, it's just before Christmas. All the seasonal shows have been cast, and there's nothing but *nothing* moving on the television front, at least until the franchise auction is settled,' or 'But my dear, it's too early in the year to be thinking of a Christmas show and it's just repeats, repeats on the telly. What do you mean

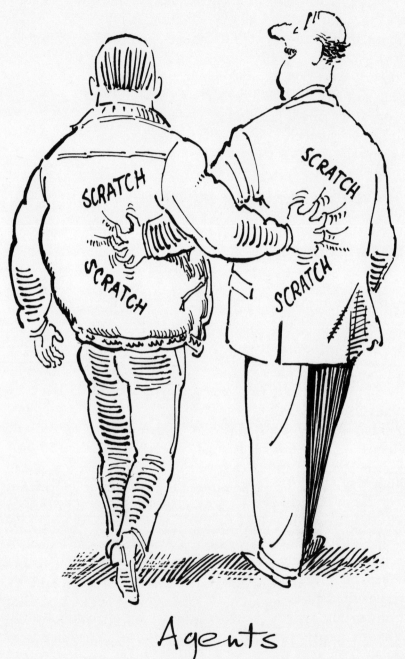

Agents

films? In this country? Darling, are you mad?' or 'But my dear, it's what, April? All the major companies are full, and you know that directors nowadays only cast people they've been to bed with, or people they are going to bed with, or people they might possibly in the future go to bed with. And you know as well as I do that television series don't start filming until a lot later in the year.' etc., etc. . . .

But let us be fair. They are stupendously and wonderfully loyal to their clients, much above considerations of where their bread is buttered. Let some raddled, spavined, broken-down old lush lumber incompetently through an execrable English farce and he will be greeted with the sort of adulation usually reserved for the return of conquering heroes. The rest of the cast may be judged utterly, but *utterly*, worthless and awful, the play itself illiterate, a load of old cliché, but despite all, like some exotic orchid on a rotting dung heap, their client is seen as something transcendentally wonderful.

Of course, it can be the case that their client is very good indeed, outshines the rest of the company and generally rises above the constraints of a mediocre script. This happened to me some years ago, when I bravely appeared in a mean-spirited and depressing play masquerading as a comedy. I divined that it was as funny as toothache on a Sunday and pitched my performance accordingly, which is to say, it was very funny indeed and, I thought, fittingly bloodless. The critics savaged the performance. The author, a sagging sensualist with the most perfectly rounded belly I'd ever seen, seemed remarkably unimpressed with my interpretation and, rather than being grateful, was profoundly depressed by the whole affair. Everyone seemed to have mistaken what I was trying to do. I was deliberately being dull and uncharismatic. What matter that it was so boring as to make people's eyes water? This was the right way, as I saw it, to present the character. I was, I must confess, a trifle dismayed at the reaction: even the *Lincoln Journal* remarked how it was a little dull; well, in fact the critic said it was the most turgid piece of non-acting she had ever witnessed. As for Sheridan Morley, that model of reserve and kindness, even he said it was rubbish. But I didn't have to despair, and I didn't. My agent thought I was wonderful. Alone in a dark world of condemnation and calumny, he stood by me and my performance. 'You old bastard,' he cried. 'You've done it again! Good isn't the word.' Even now, many years after the event, I feel my heart swell with gratitude at being told the unvarnished truth, at being recognized by at least one person as having done well. I think my agent is exceptional.

Others, it has to be said, are made of more mortal stuff and can turn quite nasty if a valuable client leaves. An agent friend of mine had a client who did just this, and from being a model of affability and a near-genius when it came to acting, overnight the client became a rogue and vagabond, a nasty, vicious person it was better not to know and someone, moreover, who lacked any shred of talent. I think the agent's hurt was compounded slightly by the knowledge that the exiting client was about to land one of the biggest and most lucrative contracts ever, but you see how transparent the behaviour of that agent was in all this. It cannot be true that this particular client changed so radically overnight from amiable, estimable thespian to offensive, amateur clod.

THE ADVERTISING EXECUTIVE

In the happy event of being offered an advert, the MC can expect to meet that exotic creature the advertising executive. This is a fellow who wears a light-grey suit and designer tie and bathes in aftershave every morning. He represents the client and his second language is English of a certain kind.

His first is Ad-speak, an extraordinary concatenation of hyperbole, circumlocution, euphemism, verbless sentences and axiomatic utterances, plucked at random from some secular bible for ad persons.

Advertising Execs

He seems perpetually on the verge of a nervous breakdown or, even worse, a heart attack. He rarely sits down but paces about, clutching a cordless telephone, sometimes stopping, always just inside your eyeline, to make hurried and furtive phone calls to other interested parties you know not of beyond the studio walls. He never talks directly to the actor, but always to the director, who's wishing he could be off doing a feature film somewhere. The director then conveys a version of what the ad person has said, though I suspect that it is a much modified version, for quite often, while the director is talking to you smilingly in a friendly fashion about an infinitesimally small adjustment they want in the performance, you can see the ad person stomping his feet and going pear-shaped in the corner, using the F word in relation to actors in general and gripping the cordless telephone as if to crush it.

He's busy covering his arse, as our American cousins would say. This scented idealist never 'commits', as the phrase is, to the advert; he always complains that nothing is right and that he is forced to settle with what he is given because of deadlines and expense. As a career move in the overheated advertising world, his attitude has much to recommend it. If the advert is a success, he will say that he 'advanced the result' despite a few snags that he ironed out; and if it is a failure, he blames those very snags or circumstances, which were of course beyond his control and not his fault.

The change in the ad person's attitude if the advert takes off is very marked indeed. Suddenly, instead of thunderous looks across an empty studio, there's an arm round the shoulder. Instead of being addressed as 'that actor' via a third person, you will find yourself within kissing distance of the smoothly shaven cheeks and called by your first name. And, moreover, you are invited to expensive executive dinners to discuss future plans in manufactured dialect which is the verbal equivalent to tinnitus – it makes no sense but it's there, and you have to try and respond.

'I'm giving my presentation in Stockholm at that time, but on return, fantastic, every chance. Brilliant overview, good specific response on the ground, plus image. We lose maybe pack shot because of the identity – it's there now – just subliminally. Eh? Fantastic. Don't go ballsing it up, like getting an anti in the News of the

Screws, ha ha ha. We can crack the code with this one, what say you?'

And so on and so on. If you want the money, flash the caps and enjoy as best you may. Remember, it's not all pleasure and titillation in the world of the MC. You have to get used to meeting many such bores.

BORES

It is a version of sod's law that many of the people who can do most for you as far as your career is concerned are more than a little earnest, not to say dull, not to say mind-numbingly boring. But the MC must learn to endure. It's all very well to have a writer as a friend, and it's even better when he promises to write you that script you so desperately want as a matter of survival, but it's not so good when you have to listen to the amiable soul telling you the plot of every novel he's ever written, those he's in the process of writing and those he's about to write. The sheer effort of smiling appreciatively through hours of turgid monologue cannot be described. The smile becomes somehow fixed, and even when you go for welcome relief to the loo, you find yourself smiling at the porcelain for it is impossible to stop.

A close thespian chum of mine discovered by accident a sort of answer to this problem, but for it to work you have to consult the weather forecast very closely and make arrangements accordingly. My friend and I used to share, here in Jersey, a rambling bungalow on one of those marvellous high headlands overlooking a vast expanse of ocean, stretching as far as the eye can see. Often times great thunderstorms would split the sky and lash the sea into a fury; the very ground would shake beneath us. We would sit in the lounge with the glass front, gaze wonderingly at the

141

spectacle and, with the aid of liberal quantities of Courvoisier, reflect on the awesome power of mother nature and our own seeming insignificance.

Bores

On such a night of storms and elemental mayhem did our writer friend arrive, and instantly embark, inevitably, on an endless monologue. I think, but I don't know for certain, that this compulsion to talk stems from the days and months that hapless scribes have to spend locked away all by themselves with nothing but a word processor for company. Once let loose from this enforced bondage and the dearth of opportunities to chat, they make up very quickly for lost time. Whatever the truth of that, here was our man with captive audience in the shape (slumped) of my friend, boring for the universe, a great lightning storm going on all around. My friend's smile became a little strained; his attention began to stray to actory things like getting BAFTA awards. He didn't wish to appear rude and suddenly hit on a masterly solution to his dilemma. He waited until our writer paused for a mini-second to draw breath and broke in quickly.

'Let's turn the lights off so we can watch the storm the better while we talk,' he said.

The writer thought this a very good idea and the lights were duly extinguished. It worked excellently. My thespian chum could dream of Oscars and doze, unobserved, quite contentedly in the periods of blackness between the great flashes of lightning, only having to sit up smartly and take notice when that lightning illumined the room for a brief second or two.

THE COMMON TOUCH

There are many ways of becoming an MC. It can be achieved by writing appalling novels about genitalia or even worse plays on the same subject. It can be achieved by going out with a Royal, though this is one of the more unpleasant ways. I don't mean that the association itself is unpleasant, but all the attendant circumstances – such as harassment at every turn by salivating hacks not averse to firing dart microphones into your house walls, the better to overhear some revealing conversation, or paying your so-called friends thousands of pounds for salacious information, or knocking you off your bike to get a better picture. One can become a celebrity (if female) by appearing on page 3 of a certain newspaper regularly and then making a few records. You can even become a celebrity, like Eddie the Eagle has done brilliantly, by failing spectacularly at everything.

Some people have been celebrities so long, the world has quite forgotten what it was that made them famous in the first place. But the vast majority of celebrities enjoy that status because they have appeared on popular television programmes. I'm talking about people like Leslie Grantham, Ian McShane, John Thaw, Rula Lenska, Mollie Sugden, John Inman and, of course, Simon Williams; the list is endless. Now, there is a major rule that all celebrities must never forget – to wit, that they should always keep the 'common' touch, like that great gift to the nation from Liverpool, Cilla Black. The lady has certainly not lost her common touch. Indeed, she is touchingly ordinary, as I can testify, being an avid watcher of *Surprise, Surprise* and that model of popular entertainment *Blind Date*.

The Common Touch!

Those people who criticize the programme for turning courting rituals into a spectator sport are surely wrong. It is always touching and funny in a very British way, and the sensitivity that Cilla brings to the presentation of the show

144

is priceless. She doesn't set herself up as superior to the contestants. She is just like them and quite unchanged by years of celebrity. Indeed, she is even more Liverpudlian now than she was back in those halcyon days when The Beatles first began. As Brian Matthews remarked on his radio programme, 'She has genuinely the common touch.' I just wish she'd sing more. But the important lesson is there for all us would-be MCs. We must never forget to be ordinary, even though, of course, many of us are anything but.

People will not appreciate it at all if an MC appears in any way snooty or patronizing, or gives himself or herself airs and graces above the ordinary. I remember in the gentle evening of a Jersey day driving Charlie Hungerford's Rolls-Royce back to its home along the winding, narrow country lanes (the regular driver had got himself lost somewhere in the vicinity of The Farmers Arms). Driving the huge car with my friend Geoffrey 'beastly' Leasley seated beside me, we were feeling very grand indeed. I even had a half-Corona stuck in my mouth. In one particularly narrow lane sloping steeply down to the beach, I observed a young paperboy, pushing his bike towards me. I brought the Rolls-Royce smoothly to a stop, the better to help the young chap go by. I pressed the little silver button and the window of the driver's seat slid quietly down. I sat there, luxuriating in the leather and cigar smoke, and thought to exchange a few words with the boy. Wouldn't he be impressed when he saw who it was had condescended to speak to him? As he drew level, he looked very hard and unsmilingly at me. 'You twat,' he said, spat vigorously and eloquently on to the ground and trudged off into the twilight.

'Beastly' Leasley appeared shocked and wished to remonstrate with the lad, but I imperiously forbade such a course of action. I had perceived instantly what had gone wrong. I had appeared too grand and condescending, too extra-ordinary and removed, to be approachable. I hadn't got that all-important common touch. The lesson was well learned. Nowadays I am always very common and very obliging. Whatever the fans want I give – photographs, books, kisses, rides in the Roadster and, of course, autographs.

As regard to these last, I am not quite so generous as that great actor Richard Pascoe. He was approached by a rather unpleasant wizened crone who used to hang round outside the theatre stage door. He was in all kinds of hurry, but stopped to give her the autograph.

'I expect you'd like Laurence Olivier's autograph as well,' he said somewhat testily.

'Oh, yes please,' she said, so Richard signed Laurence Olivier's name as well and off she went, well pleased.

FELLOW ACTORS

It is absolutely no good coming over all grand with your fellow actors, for the very simple reason that when you are forgotten and thrust back into that obscurity whence you came, they could easily be very famous indeed – which is to say, the boot could be on the other foot and you don't want to get kicked by it.

There are other equally compelling reasons to be very careful, even if you are an MC, in the treatment of your fellow artists. They can spread stories about your objectionable behaviour very quickly throughout the profession and in some bad cases you will find that actors refuse to work with you. Actors have long memories too. I remember working in my youth with a rather serious, not to say pompous, thespian – let us call him Smith – in an awful play about colonial revolution in Africa. In the course of this miserable drama, Smith, in the character of an army captain, had to die, which he did at great length and with much heaving and groaning as I held him in my arms. I was playing (even then) a lowly sergeant. On his death I had to deliver a sort of prayer over the deceased.

'My captain, I commend your soul to God and your body I must throw into the abyss. Farewell.'

At the end of that speech I would roll the inert Smith off the rostrum and he would fall out of the light on to a comfy mattress. On his expiry, Smith would slump dramatically to the floor, facing the audience, eyes open and staring, mouth dramatically agape, a thin trickle of blood from a capsule issuing forth. Understatement was a notion utterly unknown to Smith. One night, he took an even more unconscionable time a-dying – I think his wife and mother were in. He was spreading a very meagre talent very thinly indeed.

Time was pressing. Hopes of a welcome pint in the snug at The Grapes were receding, and still the egregious oaf refused to die. I could see the actors who had to come on next waiting in the wings. They had started doing the *Guardian* crossword. The way things were going, they might have finished it. Certainly, Smith was giving the audience their money's worth that night. My arms were aching with his weight. Finally, at long, long last, RADA's finest noisily expired and slumped with dramatic and certainly welcome finality to the floor facing the audience, eyes wide. I thankfully commenced on my oration over the recumbent form. Now, I admit I was hugely annoyed at such indulgence and I was very young, but really nothing could excuse my emendation of the script at this point.

'My captain, I commend your soul to God,' I began blamelessly enough, but then unforgivably and inexplicably I added, 'But now I'm going to toss you off.'

There was not a lot Smith could do because he was supposed to be dead. I held him quite still for some little time before I pushed him slowly off the rostrum. Time enough for the audience to observe Smith's face turn slowly red and then purple, the eyes close and the lips draw back across the pink teeth in a hideous grimace. The shoulders began to heave and terrifying gurgling sounds came from somewhere deep in his chest. I daresay it seemed to Smith that I held him thus dreadfully exposed for a very long time indeed, but I swear it was for no longer than one of Smith's dramatic pauses. Anyway, the fellow got very angry and surprisingly uppity about the whole rather silly incident, accusing me of being unprofessional and ruining the play. He even threatened to report me to the director. I did my best to calm him, pointing out that the writer had done a pretty good job at ruining the play long before I got to it and that the audience probably thought all Smith's convulsions and moanings were a very convincing and colourful portrayal of a man in his death throes.

Now, here I have to say that I was not helped in my attempts to calm the distraught thespian by the rest of the actors in that large communal dressing room. I don't ever like complaining about other actors' behaviour, but they really were not supportive. With scant regard for Smith's agony, they were howling with laughter and stamping up and down. It is true that a couple had the good grace to go out into the corridor so Smith could not observe them falling about, but the damage was done. The girls came crowding in from their dressing room to join in. It was all out of control and Smith was quite implacable. He never forgave me, never. All this was over fifteen years ago, but Smith has never spoken to me in all that time. He is now a famous and very excellent actor in certain parts, and was offered a rather splendid role in an episode of *Bergerac*. He turned it down flat. Not for the usual reason – lack of money – but because he didn't want to appear with me, ever. I, of course, am deeply regretful about the incident and if Smith reads this, I hope he will find it in his heart to forgive me at last.

JOURNALISTS AND THE PRESS

As an MC you, of course, welcome the attentions of all those journalists who come clamouring for your views on every subject under the sun. As that great journalist and thinker Nigel Dempster has so eloquently and so many times pointed out, the celebrity has no real right whatsoever to privacy or private life – not even on his death-bed, apparently, if Russell Harty's experiences are anything to go by. But if you are weak and feel you absolutely have to have a private life, then it will help in your dealings with the press if you remember these few ground rules.

1. Lie creatively and consistently about your personal life. I had a very long and indeed loving relationship with the same person for the past five years, but because I didn't want that person doorstepped or otherwise harassed by earnest hacks pursuing their chosen career, I never informed the press properly of the fact, *mea culpa*, merely saying I don't have time for private life. The boys from Fleet Street duly wrote this up as LONELY HEARTTHROB YEARNS FOR MISS RIGHT, or BONKLESS BERGERAC IN SEARCH FOR NEW LOVE. This approach serves a dual purpose. It preserves the privacy of your personal relationships and gives the perspiring press-man a chance to flex his alliterative muscles.

2. Make sure, if your loved one leaves you, that you have a legally binding contract with him or her that there will be no deals with any newspaper or magazine whereby a highly coloured version of your private life will be paraded for the

delectation of the British public. Don't make the mistake of thinking that this cannot happen to you – it can.

3. Make sure all members of your family are 'clean', in that they have no nasty drug habits or bizarre sexual proclivities and haven't killed anyone within living memory. It's a good career move to be very thorough as you trawl through the muddier waters of your family life, and pursue your investigation as far as you can to take in, say, uncles who live in Australia, seemingly blameless nieces in polytechnics and anyone else you can find who might be linked with you. I live in constant fear of a headline like BERGERAC COUSIN TWICE REMOVED ON HIS MOTHER'S SIDE IN SHOPLIFTING SCANDAL.

4. When a journalist closes his or her notebook, or pretends to switch off the tape-recorder, saying that the official interview is over and we can now chat freely with no risk of anything being published, then that journalist is being very penurious indeed with the truth. Of course, I would never wish to describe British journalists as congenital liars, but it would be wise to assume that they are, just as a procedural rule.

That way, you can avoid the terrible fate which befell a friend of mine. He gave an interview to a so-called freelance journalist with Antipodean connections. My friend was quite a little celebrity in that he appeared in a twice-weekly soap and he chatted of this and that to the attendant scribe. After a while, the journalist closed his notebook with a flourish and said that he had enough of what he wanted. Drinks were produced and the two fell into a lighthearted, off-the-record conversation about the other members of the soap's cast.

Now, if you work closely and intimately with people you wouldn't necessarily cross the road to spit on if they were on fire, it's sometimes therapeutic to let your hair down

151

about them and send them up behind their backs. My friend indulged himself in such a way – all, of course, in a good-natured manner. No one, but no one, escaped his caustic wit. The old father figure with the saint-like character who played the lead my friend characterized as a paunchy pae-dophile, a walking cure for insomnia who should be put out to grass. The young and pretty female lead was, according to my friend, utterly sexless, with not enough talent to clog the foot of a flea. And as for the young boy. . .

My friend went on in this vein for some considerable time, and probably felt much better for so unburdening his soul. Finally the two men parted the best of friends. They did not remain so for long. Come Sunday, the headlines told a forceful story of a soap star lashing out at the other members of the cast. All his off-the-record remarks were there, printed in bold type for everyone to see. Startling allegations indeed to read over the Rice Krispies, particularly if you yourself were appearing in that soap. My friend had perforce to go into rehearsal with all of the wonderful people he had so maligned. They wouldn't speak to him. Hell hath no fury like an actor scorned. He was excluded from the weekly visit to the Chinese restaurant. The Producer, though, did speak to him – telling him he was fired. It was a much quieter and chastened thespian who crept into the dole queue at Ladbroke Grove the following Thursday. But if we who remain can learn from his experience, then his suffering will not have been in vain.

5. If a newspaper offers to pay for a holiday for you and your girlfriend in Barbados, provided they send along a journalist and a photographer, then turn the offer down. Make any excuse you like – your skin is so fair and delicate that you can't stand the tropical sun, your agent says that you have a good chance of playing the Humphrey Bogart

role in a remake of *Casablanca*, your granny's dying – say anything but get out of it. If you accept, they will undoubtedly get you drunk and put awful words into your mouth, and it is absolutely certain that the persuasive photographer will ask you to pose for near-nude or actually nude shots. You will not have a good time. You'll have an even worse time when you get back home and see the results of their endeavours on the centre pages. Those jolly shots of you and the girlfriend, both topless, leaping about in the surf ... They seemed so right and natural at the time, but somehow in their translation to the printed page a different gloss is put on them, and was it really you who said over your sixth mug of tequila, 'I can do it six times a night.'

WOMEN ACTORS

My agent occasionally gives very good advice. It's not often this happens, but it's worth waiting for. I remember sitting in Joe Allens', trying to catch a glimpse of that greatest of MCs Christopher Biggins, when my agent told me I'd better stop rubbernecking and pay attention, as he had something of import to tell me. Word had reached him that I'd fallen in love with one of the leading ladies in the programme. How he discovered this, I am yet to learn, for certainly we had been extremely discreet about the whole affair – and, in truth, it hadn't progressed very far. My agent said that he thought the whole thing a mistake and wouldn't it be better to call a halt now, while there was still time.

I bridled at this and gave free rein over the barbecued spare ribs and very acceptable red wine to lofty sentiments concerning my right to have a decent private life, saying it was nobody's business but my own, etc., etc. My agent bore this nobly, an enigmatic smile playing round his lips. Now usually, this is a sign that he believes himself in possession

Women Actors

of a higher knowledge than is allowed us ordinary humans. This time proved no exception.

'My dear,' he began, as I finished and was burying my face self-righteously in some form of goulash. 'My dear, believe me, I couldn't care less about your private life, except –' he paused to sip a little more red wine, and then continued in those very precisely pitched and clipped tones he employs for talking from a vast height to very small boys – 'except when it interferes with your work.'

I tried to protest at this, but he raised an admonishing finger.

'Look, darling,' he said, 'I speak from bitter experience

about such things. My client –' he mentioned the name of a well-known actor who played a leading role in a ten-part series – 'my client fell in love with his leading lady during the very first episode of that series. And then they had a bitter quarrel and had separated by the third. It was all very sad, but even sadder was the fact that despite hating each other with an absolute passion, they still had to go on working together. It was an awful time for everyone and, of course, the work suffered horribly, and look, love, I think that was the reason, the real reason, why that series didn't go again. Now don't say that couldn't happen to you.'

Suddenly, I felt very humble and grateful to have such a wise person as my agent and mentor and, more than that, my friend. I forgot all about Christopher Biggins as I paid extra-special attention to the great man as he told me that he might possibly have to reconsider representing me if I persisted in such a potentially disastrous course of action. I instantly broke off the relationship and started collecting miniature trees.

THOSE WHO MAKE YOU, THOSE WHO BREAK YOU AND HOW TO BEHAVE IN THEIR COMPANY

> Lowliness is young ambition's ladder,
> Whereto the climber-upward turns his face;
> But when he once attains the utmost round,
> He then unto the ladder turns his back,
> Looks in the clouds, scorning the base degrees
> By which he did ascend.
>
> *Julius Caesar*

Not me, dear reader, nor any wise celebrity. Remember those who helped you up, for you'll surely meet them on the way down. This week's teaboy is next week's producer. This month's celebrity is next month's obituary. Today's rave review is tomorrow's chip paper. These are the curious and often hard lessons in life in the fame frame and you ignore them at your peril. In my particular branch of the entertainment industry, the producer is, of course, a highly important figure.

I have already mentioned Robert 'the Laird' Banks Stewart before, a man Terence Alexander, in conversation with Terry Wogan, called a genius. I agree. I am giving Robert a copy of this book. I admire his ability to recognize prodigious and transcendent talent when he is casting his shows. I also think it was grossly unkind of Ian McShane to try and set fire to the great man's head by use of a magnifying glass. I think Ian must regret that now, just as I regret tying a rotting cod fish to the exhaust pipe of the car belonging to a director I particularly disliked. That was very juvenile behaviour. I apologize unreservedly, the more so because I now realize that the poor man was absolutely snowed under with personal problems and was suffering a severe personality disorder, which led, among other things, to his shipping a snorting great red Trans-Am across to Jersey, which is an island only just as long as the vehicle, and casting his mates in leading parts in which they were consistently upstaged by the wallpaper.

However, it is the directors with whom your actors have most contact on a day-to-day working basis and one must be very circumspect indeed in one's dealings with them, because they are a very diverse race. Future employment may depend on their good opinion and so it is a good rule of thumb to treat them all with engaging and deferential *bonhomie*, even if you secretly believe they couldn't direct traffic from Trafalgar Square to the Houses of Parliament. More so if you believe that because, despite their awesome

Those who make you...

lack of talent, they may still go on to make important movies for cinema and television.

One such creature was employed on *Bergerac*. His inability was manifest. He was having a troubled affair with the leading lady and an even more troubled relationship with the cameraman, the soundman, the wardrobe, the make-up department, the actors – indeed, the whole world. People didn't like him one little bit. As a weary crew were walking off location after a particularly galling day's filming, some shots were heard to go off (the armourer was discharging some unused blanks into the air). The grip declared gloomily that the director had shot himself. A thespian wit instantly riposted that with the director's sense of direction, he would have missed. But, and this is the point, despite the myriad reservations about and criticisms of our benighted director, the episode was one of the best ever. The female lead went on to become deservedly (as she was an exquisitely beautiful and talented lady) a major international film star and the director, on the strength of the star, went on to work on a very major project indeed.

The reason for all this is not far to seek and I have seen this experience repeat itself many times over the years. Peter Brook, in his remarkable book *The Empty Space*, stated of theatre directors that there is only one thing better than a brilliant one, and that is an extremely bad one. In the latter circumstance, the assembled thespians will, denied the opportunity to sit back comfortably and just do as they're told, direct themselves and very often achieve excellent results. The same can be true in the world of television production, only in this case it is not just the actors who are involved: the cameraman, the sound recordists and even the gofers all join in to prevent a débâcle.

Now, most of the directors of *Bergerac* have been very

fine. Indeed, certain of them – Ben Bolt, Martin Campbell, Ian Toynton and Peter Ellis, to name but a few – were simply outstanding; but there has been a minority of another, very different kind of director. Some few years ago one of this species had such a recurring and concussive contact with the bottle that often times the left leg would start to buckle, the left eye to close, by around 2.30 in the afternoon and he would drown utterly in incoherence. One fine morning he excelled himself by not turning up at all until very late in the morning, but we managed somehow. The cameraman, the first assistant, the actors, everyone pooled their creative resources to salvage what could be salvaged, and continued to do so for the rest of this unfortunate shoot. The result was quite a good episode – not one of the very best, due to the BBC economy measure of dispensing with a writer, but a very passable effort none the less. Needless to say, the 90 per cent proof caricature of former talent got all the credit and is, even as you read this, gentle reader, directing a major cinema film somewhere in Hungary. He promised me a part in this film over dinner one night, but of course he had forgotten all about it the following morning. I hope there is not a revolution in Eastern Europe.

THE SOP FACTOR

This is a well-recorded element in the life of the MC, but it is salutary to rehearse the code of conduct relating to it. SOP stands for simple, ordinary person, a phrase which occurs very often in conversations people have with MCs. The conversation goes, 'Of course, I'm just a simple, ordinary person but ...' and then there usually follows a diatribe about how Mr or Mrs Ordinary can see what a load of old rubbish you and your programme are.

'Of course, I'm just a simple, ordinary person, nothing

SOPS

special about me, but I think ...' goes the patter; '... but I think that that character in your programme is absolutely dreadful and unbearable, just can't stand him. Of course, I'm just a simple, ordinary person, but you can't call that entertainment, and look at that Ben Elton, he's pure filth, it's just not funny. Now, I know I'm just a simple, ordinary person, but I think Max Bygraves is wonderful, but some of the stuff you see on television nowadays, I mean, I stopped watching your programme a long time ago, just can't stand it. Nothing personal, you understand, I'm just a simple, ordinary person ...'

When confronted with such talk, the MC must not lose his cool and give in to a base desire to belt the SOP straight in the dentures, even if he discovers that said SOP's greatest delight in life is listening to 'Little Donkey' performed by seven-year-olds at school nativity plays. This must not distract your MC from a fixed course of smiling acquiescence in everything the pea-brained buffoon is saying. Find some inoffensive excuse to leave – for example, you have shooting pains in your chest and have to see a doctor immediately, or you think you're going mad and want to make a will before the final blackness descends. Say anything, but leave. If you manage to do so without losing your temper, you may reward yourself liberally with a very large drink indeed – and you'll be a better man than I am.

WRINKLE-REMOVERS
Age and ageing are great problems for our society. Age and ageing are even bigger problems for your MCs, who are not expected or even allowed to grow old but must stay for ever young, or at least as young as they were when they first became famous and loved. MCs will jump through many fiery hoops to maintain the illusion that growing old and

wrinkled is an option they have deliberately turned down, and they may well behave and talk as if they were much younger than they really are.

There is an actress of my acquaintance who discovered that she was very famous at eighteen and thought to herself what a good idea it was to be eighteen, and indeed what a good idea it would be from every point of view to stay eighteen. Nowadays it is curiously frightening to be faced by this woman of forty-five, who has several chins and several children by various husbands, who wears a miniskirt like a bandage around her upper thighs, sports an impossibly coloured perm and insists on speaking in the breathy, astonished tones of a teenage virgin, untouched by human hand.

However, it is even more disconcerting to be faced by an MC who you know as a matter of record to be at least fifty years old looking a youthful thirty-five. This might be frightening, but it is indicative of the price some people will pay to stay young. Smooth surgeons all over the western world snip and tuck, cut and lift the face, shoot collagen into unyouthful wrinkles, break noses and cut through bone with razor-sharp saws to reshape the foundations. If you are fed up with aerobics, callisthenics, jogging or working out in the gym, go immediately to your friendly plastic surgeon. He will, for a price, slice out your unwanted flab, or if there is a dearth as opposed to an excess, ask him nicely and he'll put silicon implants into the vital places to make you swell and ripple according to the fashion of the day. You can stay for ever young ... for a little while.

MCs avail themselves liberally of these admirable techniques to rejuvenate, and add longevity to a career that would otherwise be destroyed too, too quickly by that old common arbitrator time. But there are certain precautions you must take. Beware the hair transplant that transplants follicles

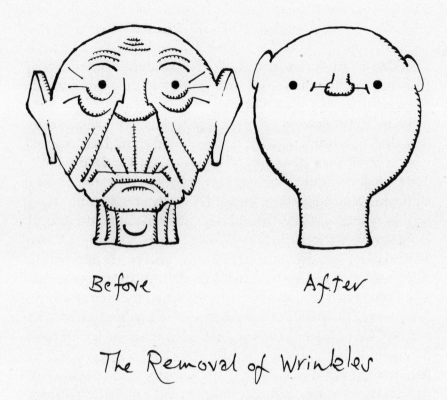

Before   After

The Removal of Wrinkles

from the back of your head to the front. Little round holes into which the implants are placed make your head look like a colander. This clearly draws unwelcome attention to that portion of your anatomy you wish not to be noticed, at least for the time being. I mean, the whole point of the painful operation is concealment of an unforgivable baldness. If people keep giggling and pointing to your pate, saying, 'Ah, his head looks like a colander. He must be sad about going bald and have had a hair transplant', then the whole purpose of the exercise is lost.

Worse, however, can follow. The hair from these implanted follicles never grows in an orderly fashion but sprouts anarchically in many different directions at once. It takes a quantity of gel or of an even more powerful fixative to force the recalcitrant strands to lie flat and in one direction.

Even then, in the more intimate, private encounters you may enjoy, the hairs have a tendency to leap up suddenly and triumphantly away from the head. This will detract from your charisma. Further, it has to be said that even when you have managed to get the hair into some reasonable order, there is never enough of it transplanted thus to create even the semblance of a full head of hair; rather, it looks like nothing so much as delicate tendrils of seaweed stretched out by a fast-racing stream. Again, people will tend not to take you seriously, so on balance this operation is best avoided.

Be careful which plastic surgeon you go to. Make sure he is a good one. Ask him to show you his portfolio of before and after pictures. The joke being told as original by at least thirty comics (though I believe Jasper Carrott was the true originator) about face lifts leaving people looking as if they are swimming at a great depth under water is eloquent of certain risks you run when you undergo such treatments, so do be careful. There was an actress in *Bergerac* who had just such an unfortunate face job – in fact, she had had quite a few face lifts over the years. The provenance of her facial skin was a total mystery. She was a lady of a certain age but in her case, dear reader, the fault was compounded: not only did she look as if she were subaquatically engaged but, more than this, she couldn't speak or even smile. The skin had been pulled up and lifted so tightly across her lower face and jaw that movement was impossible, smiling was impossible and speech became impossible. Her dilemma must have been painful indeed: appear ten years younger but be silent and look perpetually miserable, or look your age but be able to grumble about it. These are hard decisions the ageing MC will have to consider seriously, and it is best to pay for the best and avoid the hack and heave brigade.

If, however, your face is beginning to look like a relief

map of the Lake District and you don't want to go to the expense or indeed the discomfort of plastic surgery, the Americans have invented a clever little gadget which lifts the face and eliminates the jowl effect quite effectively, if temporarily. I have tried this cunning contraption and can vouch for its efficacy. It is a thin, curved and adjustable piece of plastic or metal with two small pieces of strong adhesive affixed to either end. The *modus operandi* is to place the curved plastic or metal strip across the top of the head, cleverly concealing it in the hair (this contraption does not work at all for a bald person). The two pieces of adhesive are attached firmly to the skin just in front of the ears and then the strip can be shortened, so lifting the skin around the lower face and jaw. Continue until you are satisfied that you look beautiful. This is such a simple device that I daresay you could make one yourself, if you were so inclined, simply by replacing the actual earphones on a Walkman headpiece and replacing them with two pieces of Sellotape.

But remember, as an American doctor pointed out to me, that continuing to appear for ever youthful is an absolute commitment. You cannot stop at the hair or even the face. It is no good having the face of a twenty-year-old if your body is a mess and looks like an ill-packed sack of Jersey potatoes. Now, I know the doctor was touting for trade, but he was speaking a lot of sense. Don't think just the face, go the whole distance. Think positive. Have a body lift.

NEVER BELIEVE YOUR OWN PUBLICITY – YOU LIVE WITH YOURSELF; YOU KNOW IT'S NOT TRUE

Furthermore, never believe your own publicity when it comes to doing your own show, particularly if you are popularly described as 'hunky, heroic, brave and fearless'. Forget all that when you go out in front of the camera. If anything

looks remotely dangerous get a stuntman or stunt double to
do it for you. This is a very good thing for two reasons: a)
they need the money, and b) they can do it much better than
you. Of course, as the hero of a television cops and robbers
show, you must never own up in public to not having done
your own stunts, but I can tell you – in confidence of course –
how to tell when a stuntman has taken over from the invin-
cible blue-eyed hero to fall down cliffs, get clouted with
suspiciously delicate pieces of furniture, or ride viciously
powerful motorbikes.

The first indication is that the face is turned away from
the camera. This is proof positive, for no actor – unless he
is deranged, appearing in a soap with no street cred, or is
practising a subtle form of tax avoidance – will turn his or
her face away from the camera willingly. I have observed
actors, usually such kind and chivalrous creatures, literally
fight each other to get their face full frontal into the camera.
It is rumoured that in that great hymn to social realism,
Dallas, the actors who are supposed to be acting to each other
in a scene, very often record their performances separately on
their own to camera, thus avoiding unpleasant scenes of the
kind just mentioned.

The stuntman, however, cannot of necessity court the
camera in this way for if he does, it immediately becomes
clear that he is not the hero the audience expect to see, but
somebody entirely different. The make-up department must
make and generally does make some attempt to make your
stunt double look as much like you as possible. It is no good,
as happened in *Yellowthread Street*, your actual six foot fair-
haired blue-eyed Caucasian hero thundering through some
oriental city street on a suspiciously high motorbike, turning
into a small black-haired Chinese person when he crashes
into a stall, does three back flips and one forward roll to land

I never believe my own publicity.

Or any sort of publicity!

perfectly positioned to overpower the baddie. The great British public will quickly observe that a substitution has been made.

The stunt double must wear the same clothes as the hero he is standing in for and have at least the same colour hair. Now the hair should not be difficult – a well fitted wig will do the trick and the clothes can be the same ones as our hero wears, or an identical outfit. The major problem I have found with stuntmen is that they tend to be rather large, rather tough gentlemen, possessed of infinitely more bulk than your average thespian who generally speaking, has spent most of his life cloistered away from the public gaze, pursuing a life of gentle dissipation which is aesthetically pleasing but doesn't promote the development of a lot of muscle.

Here then is another major indication that the leading man has been replaced, the sudden, nay instantaneous acquisition of huge shoulders and biceps, the acquisition of a powerful bull neck as opposed to the swanlike variety which is the property of the hero and the concomitant ability to perform feats of athleticism, not taught at RADA. The cameraman may help here to create the illusion that it really is our hero who is performing deeds of derring-do, by creating a long shot slightly out of focus of the action so it becomes virtually impossible to make a positive identification of the protagonists. The stuntmen can throw themselves about (literally) in the sure knowledge that they won't be recognized.

One of the best stunts I ever saw was when a stunt double ran along the extended arm of a huge crane about 120 feet up and plunged off the end to dangle suspended in mid-air on a rope wrapped around one ankle. I could not watch. Neither could the fellow he was standing in for, an Irishman with a taste for wine at lunchtime, a terrific, nay outstanding integrity but absolutely no head for heights. Immediately prior to the stunt sequence along the arm of the crane, he and I had to do an extended fight on a small service gantry about ninety feet up. This was formed from grating through which one could see the ground. There was a low safety rail about three feet high running around it. It was a somewhat unnerving and vertiginous experience to leap on to that little grating and pretend to fight. My Irish friend had lunched well and imbibed not a little of the vino collapso of dubious vintage and provenance purveyed in screwtop bottles. It was an exceedingly hot day. Wearing a heavy suit, tie and a rather preposterous wig, he was perspiring freely. His colour was ashen beneath the makeup. He would not, absolutely *not*, have a stunt double for the sequence. This was a mistake. He leapt on to the grating and did the sequence. He did very well and sat down off the crane at the end, lit a cigarette, almost sobbing with relief. Unfortunately for him, indeed for us all, there was a technical fault with the camera and so the whole thing had to be repeated. This was far too much. The poor chap got half-way through then his nerve broke, he turned away from me with strange strangulated grunts, fell to his knees, leaned over the safety rail and was violently sick. People standing the ninety or so feet below did not seem much pleased with this gift from heaven, but they moved very quickly indeed out of range, shouting remarks I could not quite make out. Two electricians near to me, betraying an unusual insensitivity, were trying to guess which of the three or four choices our cooks had offered for lunch the poor man had actually eaten. We all joined in but no consensus was achieved. The Irishman went home very sad. The moral of this tale is not too far to seek – if in doubt, use a stuntman.

However, there are occasions when your MC is required to do more than pose fetchingly around the set looking pretty, and one such occasion occurred some ten years ago in an episode of *Bergerac* which required myself and an actor chum to do just a little bit of abseiling on the high cliffs at Les Landes. Now I get vertigo on a deep pile carpet, and was not looking forward to this experience at all, but the jolly stuntmen – and there were a lot of them – assured me it was OK.

It was a drizzly sort of a day and the ropes were wet and slippery. This did not increase my confidence. My fellow actor however seemed to be all right, chatting and joking with the crew. He was and is a very large man, upwards of eighteen stone, with a girth as large as his talent, which is to say, considerable. Towards the end of the day it was at last our turn to be dropped over the cliff face in close up. I gritted my teeth and held on tight, not daring to look down at all. I tried to occupy my mind with other thoughts. I tried to think of all my good reviews together but this didn't take very long so I thought of how much I was getting paid to do this ridiculous stunt, which didn't work either. The money didn't seem in any way commensurate to the risk. I hung on for dear life and for what seemed like an eternity. Finally they hauled me up. I tried for a nonchalant attitude but failed miserably. My hand shook as I tried to light a cigarette, I said it was the cold, even though the sweat was running in rivulets down my face. Now it was my large friend's turn. He stood poised at the very edge of the cliff. The camera was rolling. 'Cut' called the stuntman who had fortunately noticed that the safety line was slack to the point that if the actor had fallen, he would have been smashed to pieces on the rocks below. That fault corrected, the great man lowered himself down the precipitous cliff face after we exchanged a few words of dialogue. During this exchange and while he was going over the cliff, I thought I observed signs if not

170

quite of fear then certainly of apprehension flit across his features. True it wasn't the eyes closed, jeloid terror that I had shown, but it was a species of definite concern. Nevertheless, he completed the shot in fine style and we sat together on the rough heather afterwards to reminisce about our experiences at the end of the rope.

'Were you a bit nervous?' I inquired. 'Did the bottle go a bit?'

The brave fellow admitted as much. 'But why,' said I. 'I thought you'd said you'd abseiled before?'

'Yes,' he replied, 'But only upwards.'

THE PHILOSOPHY OF CELEBRITY
A serious word here. A great literary figure of my acquaintance once put his arm around my shoulder in kindly fashion and gave me the benefit of his years of experience as a major celebrity, lionized and fêted in the capitals of the world. I felt much as Plato must have felt sitting at the feet of Socrates, and I will pass on to you, dear reader, some of his wisdom in the hope that you will benefit from it as I certainly have over the years.

Fame, he told me gravely, was being invited to dinner by royalty one minute and being totally unrecognized by a hotel receptionist the next. Yes, yes I could see that, though my experience had been precisely the opposite in that though I have never been invited to dinner by royalty, I am often recognized by hotel receptionists. But I could see that in the great man's scheme of things the two parties were interchangeable.

Furthermore, he imparted to me the news that people would try and take advantage of me by asking for money. Yes, yes I could see that too, but that could only surely be a matter of degree for Julian (I forbear to tell you his second

171

name for the case is still *sub judice*) borrowed perpetually from me when I was in rep in Bristol and as obscure as Bernard Manning's charisma. Still I could see that if I had more people would ask for more but then I didn't particularly mind that for I enjoyed being able to give to really needy people like my tax inspector who, I suspect, has been forced to watch *Bergerac* too often for my own good.

My friend then led me gently toward the chuck wagon and even more importantly toward the appreciation of the most secret truths of even minimal celebrity: 'People don't love you for what you are,' he confided, gazing dreamingly into the middle distance, 'but what you appear to be on their screens. Now I am not saying you yourself are untalented. I wouldn't presume to judge, but nothing is more common today than successful men with no talent, if I may paraphrase that great philosopher Ray Kroc; I mean that success and celebrity do not necessarily depend on talent in these dog days and it is a good thing that you never ever believe it does, otherwise you might miss out on the joke of the century.'

The Philosophy of Celebrity

Epilogue

I was perplexed mightily as a child by the parable of the talents. You know, the one about the rich man who goes into a far country and gives one servant five talents, another two and a third, one. The one with five invests his talents and gets more for his pains. The second servant likewise invests his two talents and gets a 100 per cent return, but the third fellow goes and digs in the earth and hides his one talent. When the master returns he rewards the first two servants lavishly for their endeavours, but the third he casts out with nothing, saying that everyone who has shall be given more and will have abundance, while he who does not have, even that which he has will be taken from him. This always struck me as a litle unfair, not to say harsh. Why should the fellow with a lot get even more? Why should the understandably fearful chap, who has too little to risk playing the market, be deprived of even that which he has kept intact?

Mr Rundle, our saturnine RC teacher of unimpeachable holiness, long of nose and short of stature, ruminated that

Epilogue

the secret of understanding this somewhat opaque tale lay in the use of the word talent, which he saw as a kind of pun, referring at one and the same time to both a sum of money and, more importantly, an ability or aptitude. If you wasted your talents or abilities by not exploring and expressing them to their full extent, then they would atrophy and die and be indeed cast out from you.

So said the monkish Rundle, and possibly with some truth, but I don't think so. I think the parable was simply and very accurately describing the world of the MC. The less fame you have, the sooner you will be hustled off into the encircling gloom, to be forgotten. On the other hand, the more fame and celebrity you possess, the more of almost everything you will get. It's unfair, I agree, but that is the way the star cookie crumbles. I don't need the meals to be free when I go to wonderful restaurants like Chikakos in Bath or the Taj Mahal at La Pulente (well, I did say I would mention them), and I don't need free seats at theatres, or free flights to exotic parts of the world. Of course, I appreciate them all tremendously, but I cannot say with my hand on my heart that I need them to be free because I, and most other of my fellow MCs, can quite easily afford to pay for them. But nice people keep insisting we do not. Paradoxical it may be, but symptomatic of our mad world.

I expect there will be an end one day (but not yet, O Lord, not yet) and I will have finished enjoying the delights of strutting and spinning on the celebrity roundabout, and I will go the way of hundreds of others before me into the restful obscurity of untroubled age, leaving the world not quite to darkness but to even more MCs to dance their measures before an appreciative crowd. And that is as it is and as it should be.

Nudity in a Public Place

Time is like a fashionable host
That slightly shakes his parting guest by the hand,
And with his arms outstretched, as he would fly,
Grasps in the comer: welcome ever smiles,
And farewell goes out sighing.

Troilus and Criseyde

Whether the sighs will be of regret or of relief I leave you, dear reader, to judge.